Joy for the

Preacher

Book Five

Small Town

Matchmaker

Cheryl Wright

Joy for the Preacher
(Book Five, Small Town Matchmaker)

Copyright 2023 by Cheryl Wright

Small Town Romance Publications

Dedication

To Margaret Tanner, my very dear friend and fellow author, for her enduring encouragement and friendship.

To Alan, my husband of over forty-eight years, who has been a relentless supporter of my writing and dreams for many years.

To You, my wonderful readers, who encourage me to continue writing these stories. It is such a joy knowing so many of you enjoy reading my stories as much as I love writing them for you.

Table of Contents

Chapter One

Crystal Springs, Montana – 1880s

Preacher Clyde Walters sat at his desk working on his next sermon. He enjoyed the quiet humming coming from the church as the ladies readied the flowers for the service. A smile creased his lips and the words simply flowed.

Family, friendship, and community. That would be his message on Sunday. Not that the townsfolk here needed to be reminded. Crystal Springs was a very close-knit community. They came to the rescue when help was needed and ensured no one went without.

Each of the stores in town donated to the Ladies Auxiliary every week, and did whatever they could do. The people of the town were equally generous, donating what they could afford. Not everyone in Crystal Springs had it easy. Several were on the verge of poverty. It was his job to ensure his flock were looked after—even those who never found their way to his services.

Suddenly, the humming he'd enjoyed so much stopped, and Clyde heard the church door close. The ladies must be finished. It was a shame, since he was enjoying the sound, even if it was a little out of tune. Suddenly, the words of "Onward Christian Soldiers" rang out. This was new. It was also a voice he didn't recognize.

The preacher was tempted to hurry to the vestry door and check out who was singing. The sudden change of pace intrigued him, and he wondered which of their wonderful volunteers had such an amazing voice. He also wondered why he'd never heard it before.

Placing his pencil on the desk, he pushed back his chair as quietly as he could, in order not to disturb the owner of that beautiful voice. Perhaps he could convince her to sing in church one day?

Clyde knew he was being selfish now. Enjoying the music this lovely volunteer produced was one thing. Convincing her to sing publicly was another thing altogether. He believed everyone should share their God-given talents, but they were not all confident enough to do so.

He stepped quietly over to the door and glanced about. Two women had their backs to him, diligently wiping down the pews and straightening the Bibles. Molly Ryan, the doctor's wife, he knew.

But who was the other woman? The one with the incredible voice?

Molly glanced up at him, a wide smile on her face. "Clyde," she called across the room. "I hope we didn't disturb you?" She frowned at her last words.

"Not at all, Molly. I was enjoying the beautiful sound that echoed through our wonderful church," he said. "Was that you singing?"

Molly laughed. "Not at all. I wish I had a voice as beautiful as that." She motioned to the other woman, standing not far away. "It was my cousin, Faith. She's come to stay with Marcus and me for a while." Molly's laughter disappeared as quickly as it had arrived. It made Clyde wonder if the cousin was in some sort of trouble. He shook himself mentally. Surely, he was overreacting. He didn't even know this woman.

The preacher watched as the newcomer sighed. Her shoulders went down as quickly as they'd risen, then she slowly turned to face him. There was little sign of happiness on her face, and yet, her voice betrayed her mood right now.

By the time she faced him completely, a small smile tugged at her lips. She stepped forward with her hand outstretched. "I'm pleased to meet you, Preacher Walters. Molly has told me all about you."

He did not know why, but Clyde was certain the woman was hiding something. Or perhaps she was hiding. He again mentally shook himself. Why he was getting a feeling of foreboding, he had no idea. Glancing across at Molly for reassurance, he found none. She was studying the floor.

Faith pulled out of his grip almost the moment their hands touched. He studied her. She wasn't short, far from it. She'd pulled her long blonde hair up into a bun, presumably to keep it out of her face while she worked. But the thing that really caught his attention was her striking blue eyes. They seemed tinged with sadness, and he wanted to know why.

"Welcome to Crystal Springs. I hope you're enjoying your time here." At his words, Faith glanced across to Molly, then bit her bottom lip. "Thank you for helping with the cleaning and the flowers. We always appreciate it."

"I don't mind at all," Faith said, then turned to Molly. "Always happy to help my cousin."

The women exchanged a look. Clyde couldn't quite put his finger on it, but was certain they were concealing something. "How long are you staying?" he asked.

Again, Faith turned to Molly as if looking for reassurance. "We don't know yet," Molly said quickly. "Right now it's undecided." The women shared a glance again. It got stranger and stranger by the minute.

"However long you stay," the preacher said, "I hope you enjoy your time here. Perhaps I'll see you at the service on Sunday?"

"Most likely," Faith answered, then went back to cleaning the church.

Clyde returned to the vestry and his upcoming sermon, but curiosity plagued him. Something was definitely going on. Whether he got to the bottom of it was debatable.

Sadly, the singing did not continue.

As he finished writing his sermon, Clyde stood and stretched. He'd sat there for quite some time. While the interruption of meeting Molly's cousin was a pleasant one, it put him behind. Now he needed a coffee. He stopped as he heard movement in the church.

Were the women still there? After all this time? It was unimaginable—he'd been working on his sermon for well over an hour, and that was since his curiosity had been piqued. Just as he'd done before, Clyde moved to the open door of the vestry that led into the church and glanced about.

If not for the slightest movement, he would have missed her. In the middle of the church, on one pew, sat Faith, Molly's cousin. This time, she was alone. She seemed to pray, but perhaps she was only contemplating…what he didn't know.

Clyde moved as quietly as he could, in an endeavor to leave Faith to her solitude. The church was never closed, the doors never locked, and she was free to come and go as she pleased. In his mind, it was the way it should be. People should have the opportunity to pray and to praise God whenever they wanted, or indeed, needed, to do so. That had been a long held belief of his.

"Preacher." Faith's sweet voice invaded his thoughts. "Did I interrupt you again? I apologize."

Frowning, Clyde stepped toward her. "Not at all," he said. "Nor did you interrupt previously. I enjoyed your singing." It was calming, very soothing, and he'd welcomed it. He glanced about, but couldn't see Molly.

"Molly left. Her parents were bringing little Joey back home after a visit."

The thought had Clyde smiling. The town had come to life with all the marriages and babies that had ensued. It was something he'd prayed about for a very long time. Dennis Andrews was the instigator of most of the marriages. Even if his matchmaking ways had irritated some of the town's people.

The very thought had Clyde chuckling. "What's so funny?" Faith asked, a smile tugging at her lips. For the first time, he stared into her face, and really studied it. Apart from her striking eyes, her face was round. The woman was far from petite, and he had no doubt she could look after herself. He hoped she didn't need to do that.

Once again, his curiosity was piqued. Molly hadn't mentioned any of her cousins would come visiting. Not that he suspected she would. But it all seemed rather cloak and dagger to him. "I was thinking about the town matchmaker and how none of our youngsters would exist if it wasn't for that annoying man." He grinned then, and Faith's smile lit up her face. "Would you like refreshments?" Where those words came from, Clyde didn't know, but he knew he wanted to spend time with this intriguing woman. Merely to find out her story, he convinced himself. "We can go to the diner," he said. "I would not put you in a compromising position." And he wouldn't. A preacher, of all people, knew what happened when women were compromised—they were forced to marry the man in question. Even if that was not what they wanted.

Faith stood then. "It sounds lovely," she said.

Clyde offered his arm, and she accepted. They headed out to the diner. He was looking forward to her company.

Chapter Two

Faith sat opposite the preacher in the diner.

As Molly had promised, Crystal Springs was quiet. The people seemed nice, and the preacher was special. He was a gentleman, and his compassion was obvious. The preacher back home was worlds apart from Preacher Walters. He wanted her to... No, she wouldn't go there.

"Tea for the lady, and coffee for you, Preacher." The waitress placed their drinks in front of them, as well as a plate of assorted muffins in the center of the table. "Is there anything else I can get you?"

The preacher glanced at Faith, and she shook her head. This was far too much already.

"That's it, thank you," he said, a smile on his face, then indicated for Faith to help herself to a muffin. "Ladies first."

She hadn't felt hungry, but the aroma coming from the still warm muffins sitting in front of her changed all that. She reached for a blueberry muffin. "Thank you, Preacher Walters," she said.

He frowned. "Clyde, please. Few people call me by my Christian name, and sometimes I forget I even have one." He laughed then, and Faith couldn't help but laugh with him. He chose a lemon muffin and took a bite. "Delicious," he said, although she could tell from his expression alone he was enjoying it.

It made her wonder how often he treated himself. At first Faith thought he'd brought her here to spoil her, but now she wondered if it was for them both. He certainly seemed to savor that muffin. Until now, she hadn't taken a bite, but was now eager to do so. How could baked goods have that effect on a person?

"I take it you don't eat here very often?" she asked, then chewed on her bottom lip. That came out completely wrong. Almost derogatory.

Instead of being annoyed, he grinned. "It's that obvious?" He laughed then. "I come to the diner. This is a rare, but very pleasant occasion."

Their eyes met, and Faith knew this was not what it seemed. Not to her, and perhaps not to the preacher sitting opposite her. It was far more than that. She also knew neither of them would take it further.

Besides, she would leave here as soon as things settled down back home. Then she would return to her normal life.

She sighed. Faith wondered if that was even possible. Instead of thinking about her troubles, she enjoyed the company of this likeable man of the cloth. He seemed lonely, and she was in a state of confusion. Spending time together was likely what they both needed.

Faith smiled. Warmth flooded her as she brought the teacup to her lips. Clyde followed suit, and she vowed to make the most of her time with him before she went back to Marcus and Molly's home.

They walked arm in arm as the preacher escorted her home. Strangely enough, Faith felt comforted by his presence. And safe. She hadn't felt that way for a very long time. Until she'd arrived to visit her cousin. Even then, there was an element of unrest.

Marcus had promised to protect her, and Faith knew he would, but unease seemed to follow her everywhere. Except in the company of Preacher Clyde Walters. He had an aura about him, and he made her feel special. Even wanted, but definitely comforted.

She shook herself mentally. That's what preachers did—it was their job to ensure they put their parishioners at ease. Their troubles lessened. Wasn't it?

Of course it was. She knew it was true. But she wasn't one of his parishioners—she was a complete stranger to this man.

Had he sensed something was eating away at her? She'd almost blurted it out when he'd approached her in the church. After Molly had left.

She'd sat alone, praying for salvation. For a way out of the predicament she was in. Instead, God had sent the preacher along to comfort her with his presence. It was a start, but she would need to pray harder to find redemption. Would she confess all to the preacher? Faith thought not, but one should never discount the truth.

After all, her sins were not easily washed away. It would take a lot for her to receive forgiveness, and she doubted she ever would.

"Well, here we are," the preacher told her, sounding reluctant to leave. "I'll see you again?" he asked, and Faith wondered if he was genuinely interested or merely being polite. She was not interested in a relationship of any type. Faith was in Crystal Springs to spend time with Molly and her family. She was enjoying their company and couldn't get enough of sweet little Joey.

Faith glanced up at him. "I believe I'll be here for a few more days. Perhaps longer." She bit her lip then. More likely than not she would slip away unnoticed, although now it seemed like a terrible idea. It felt as though she was lying to a man of the cloth, and that didn't bode well.

"You'll keep in touch?" He shook his head then. "Maybe I'll see you at church on Sunday." Clyde stared at her momentarily, then walked back the way he'd come.

As she watched him retreat, Faith felt bereft. Her heart sank—she'd lied to the man walking away from her. He might be a preacher, a man of God, but he was still a person with feelings and needs. "Clyde," she called out suddenly. He turned to face her, a smile on his face, and her heart fluttered. "If you are free tomorrow, perhaps we could go for a stroll."

The smile turned into a huge grin.

Faith opened the door and went inside, warmth filling her. Already she wanted to stay in Crystal Springs, for no other reason than to spend time with the preacher.

She wondered if she'd unwittingly committed yet another sin.

Clattering from the kitchen enticed her further inside. Molly was at the stove, and Joey sat on the floor playing with pots and pans. Marcus would be tending to his patients.

Molly turned to face her. Her smile quickly disappeared. She studied Faith, worry replacing her previous expression. "Are you alright? You appear... confused." She indicated for Faith to sit at the table. Molly sat too.

"The preacher took me to the diner." Her heart fluttered at the memory. Molly grinned, and without her saying as much as a word, it was clear her cousin was happy at this turn of events. She was suddenly suspicious. "Did you set me up?" she asked warily. After everything that had occurred, Faith didn't think Molly would do such a thing.

Molly appeared shocked. "I didn't, I promise. You deserve some happiness in your life, even if it's only short term." Joey handed her a pan, and Molly smiled again. "I can't understand why you would even contemplate going back home." She turned to face her young son, then lifted him into her arms.

Faith watched the pair interact. She had always wanted a family. After what she'd endured, it didn't seem something that would happen. Not ever. Molly kissed Joey's forehead, then put the boy back to the floor. "I need to attend to supper," she said, and stood. "I'm always available to talk."

"Thank you. I know," Faith whispered. "I'll freshen up," she said, then left the room. She came here to get her thoughts in order. And to get away... No, she wouldn't think about that. Preacher Clyde Walters had sent her mind into disarray, and now Faith wasn't sure what to do.

She shook her head as she headed toward the bathroom at the end of the long hallway. This was merely a side effect of... everything. He was a preacher, for goodness' sake! Faith was not interested in a relationship, and she was certain he wasn't either. Besides, she'd known the man for less than two hours. He wouldn't have any such thoughts. Faith was positive about it.

Chapter Three

Clyde strolled back to the church, a noticeable skip in his step.

He liked Faith. Not that it was surprising—there were few people he didn't like. It was a pity she wasn't staying in town. She would fit in perfectly. Molly and Faith were much alike. They both had a pleasant personality, and from the little he knew of Faith, she was a caring person. Not unlike her cousin.

Clyde couldn't help but smile. It had been a long time since he'd felt this way. Of course, he enjoyed interacting with his parishioners. That was a given. The townsfolk in Crystal Springs were amongst the best people he knew. Kind, caring, and always willing to help. It's what made him want to stay here long term. Some of his previous postings had been more than a little challenging. A few had been downright dangerous.

But Crystal Springs was different. It felt like home almost the moment he'd arrived. As he reached the church, he glanced across at the mercantile. He needed a few supplies, including for supper. The thought made him pause. Dennis was always trying to find a match for him.

At least the preacher knew he wasn't alone. Dennis was bored, he was certain. Anyone who lived in this town was lucky if they avoided Dennis's matchmaking ploys. The man was a pest, but most people simply didn't take him seriously.

He crossed the road, then stalled as he reached for the handle. Dennis didn't miss much—the man was matchmaker and busybody all rolled into one. Clyde sighed, then opened the door, the bell over the door shattering the peacefulness of the town.

"Good afternoon, Preacher," Dennis said with a grin on his face. "Who is the young lady?"

It was all Clyde could do to stop himself from rolling his eyes. Still, he shouldn't get mad at the man. His store was in the perfect position to see whatever happened in this town. "She is Molly Ryan's cousin. Faith is only here for a few days." There. That should appease the store owner's curiosity.

The other man's shoulders slumped. It seemed Dennis was up to his usual tricks, but his plan had been thwarted. Clyde held back a grin. "A bag of tea, if you don't mind, Dennis," he said firmly, trying to pull the man's attention away from matchmaking. "I'd best get a bag of biscuits, too.

For the vestry," he added, in case Dennis thought he was entertaining Faith. The man was incorrigible and who knew what went through his mind?

Dennis wrote the preacher's purchases into his account book. "Will that be all?"

What had Clyde been thinking? "Do you have any sausages? I need something for supper." He heard a soft chuckle from Dennis.

"For one or two?" Dennis asked, his face now serious.

If he didn't need the supplies, he would have stormed out right that moment. "Dennis Andrews…" the preacher began, then stopped himself. There was no point in getting angry with the man. He silently prayed for forgiveness, and for patience. Some days, Dennis was simply too much.

"Yes, Preacher?" Dennis had an expression of innocence, but Clyde knew the man was far from that.

"I'll take six sausages and half a dozen eggs. Do you have any bacon? Four pieces will do, thank you." A sly smile appeared on Dennis's lips. "That will see me through two nights. After that, I guess I'll be back," he added quickly, hoping it wiped the smile off the matchmaker's lips.

It had the desired effect.

"Thank you for your custom," Dennis said as Clyde left the store. He breathed a sigh of relief the moment he was out on the boardwalk. What he needed was to work out his supplies for a week, or even a month. That way, he wasn't affected by Dennis several times a week.

He knew Dennis was lonely. All the signs were there. With loneliness often came unhappiness, then bitterness set in. Although he couldn't say the store owner came across as bitter. There was, however, no doubt in Clyde's mind that Dennis needed a wife. The matchmaker needed someone to match *him* up.

The thought had Clyde chuckling all the way across the road.

As he unlocked the door to the parsonage, the house felt uncharacteristically empty. He'd done this so many times before and never had this feeling of hollowness. It wasn't often he entered this way; he acknowledged that. Most of the time, he entered via the church. Taking Faith to the diner offered a rare break from his routine.

Of course, he visited his house-bound parishioners, but apart from that, he rarely socialized. Not in the true sense of the word. He was occasionally invited to dine with members of his church, but on the whole, he was a loner. Besides, getting to know his flock on a personal level could make it more difficult if he needed to help them.

Now in his kitchen, Clyde set about placing all the items where they belonged. Tea went into the canister, biscuits in another container, and the perishable items were placed in the icebox. It was then he realized his milk was getting low.

He shrugged. Clyde was not going back to the mercantile today. Dennis had already gotten under his skin, and that was enough for one day.

The knock at the front door startled him. Walking down the hallway to the front of the house, his footsteps echoing, made Clyde even more aware of how empty his home was. He wondered why he'd never noticed it before.

He opened the door to find Faith standing there. Molly was also there, with young Joey in a stroller. Faith gazed at him, a smile on her face.

"Oh!" Clyde said, pleasantly surprised at his visitors. "What can I do for you ladies?"

Faith smiled. "We wondered if you'd like to come for supper?" She opened her eyes wide in anticipation. Did that mean she would be pleased to have his company? Had Faith enjoyed their time together at the diner?

He shook himself mentally. It wasn't like they'd been on a date. He'd merely wanted sustenance, and invited Faith to join him. That's what he told himself, anyway.

"We would love to have you join us," Molly said from behind Faith. Craning his neck, Clyde noticed the grin on little Joey's face, the boy now in his mother's arms.

"I've bought sausages for supper," he said matter-of-factly. "I've literally just finished putting them in the icebox."

The smile on Faith's face disappeared. "Sausages? You call that supper?" She shook her head. "That will never do, Clyde, and we both know it. Molly has a delicious stew cooking. There's far more than three adults can eat. You'd be helping us out," she said, her voice almost pleading.

He knew he shouldn't, but Clyde took offense at Faith's comment about sausages. "I put eggs and bacon with the sausages," he said gruffly. "There's nothing wrong with that." He looked at Molly then. Surely she would back him up.

"I agree with my cousin," she said instead. "I couldn't live with myself knowing you are eating such a meal." She placed Joey back in the stroller and turned toward her home. "We'll see you at five thirty."

Without another word, the trio headed toward home, leaving Clyde to wonder what had occurred.

It wasn't bad enough Dennis was trying to match him up. Now he was being manipulated by two women. He acknowledged they probably meant well, but his day had been interrupted, not to mention his meal plans, and Clyde wasn't sure where it would lead.

Chapter Four

"What else needs to be done?" Faith asked, glancing about the kitchen. She wanted everything to be perfect. She wasn't certain why she felt that way, other than the preacher seemed lonely. That he had strolled out of the vestry in the middle of composing his sermon, to listen to her singing, told her a lot.

The moment he'd entered the church, something had come over her. If she had to explain it, she wasn't sure she could. A peacefulness had surrounded her. Of course, she'd been in a church and that was a given.

"I think that's everything," Molly said. "Clyde should be here any minute."

"If he doesn't back out, you mean?" Faith chuckled. Molly glanced across at her, a frown on her face. It made Faith wonder if he actually would turn up. "He wouldn't stand us up, would he?"

Molly paused for long enough to cause Faith to worry. "No, I'm sure he wouldn't. Clyde has always been reliable. And he's a man of his word. He accepted the invitation, so I'm certain he'll come."

"He didn't actually accept," Faith said, recalling their conversion. Faith couldn't help herself. She let out a long sigh of relief. Moments later, there was a knock at the door. Footsteps in the hallway told her Marcus headed that way. Once the door opened, muffled voices followed, along with Joey's excited voice. More likely than not, her little cousin was cradled in his doting father's arms.

"He's here!" Faith suddenly gasped. She glanced about again, taking in the entire room and trying to assess if anything else was needed.

"Don't panic. Everything is ready." Molly's calm voice was reassuring.

As much as Faith knew she was panicking, she didn't want to admit it. Nor did she understand why she felt this way. According to Molly, having the town's preacher to supper was not an unusual occurrence. It was no different to the sheriff, who was also often invited to supper. The townsfolk appreciate the effort men in those positions put in, and it was their way of thanking them.

Besides, Marcus and Clyde were friends.

With her back to the kitchen door, Faith felt eyes on her. She spun around to find Clyde standing there, watching the activity. "Good evening, ladies," he said. "Thank you again for inviting me."

Although he addressed them both, his eyes never left Faith. Heat traveled from her neck to her cheeks, and she turned back to the tray of biscuits she'd moments ago removed from the oven. She continued to place them on a platter, and then, taking a sustaining breath, turned back to face him. "Good evening, Clyde," she said, and stepped across the room to place the platter on the table where they would all share a meal.

"I'll put Joey down before we eat," Molly said, then added, "he's already eaten, and as you can see from the way he's rubbing his eyes, he's tired." Marcus handed the boy over, and Molly left the room.

Faith was pleased Marcus was still there. She wasn't sure what to say to the preacher, who was really a stranger to her. But then again, they'd spent time together earlier in the day and she'd felt completely relaxed in his company. Why was she feeling so anxious now?

"Please," Marcus said as he motioned toward the table. "Take a seat, Clyde. Molly won't be long."

"Thank you. I truly appreciate the invitation. Your Molly is such an excellent cook, too." He smiled then, something he didn't often do, and Faith felt warmth flood her—from her head to her toes. "Have you decided how much longer you will be in Crystal Springs?" he asked Faith.

Faith wasn't sure how to answer. "Another day or two, perhaps? I haven't really decided."

Clyde nodded, and he seemed a little disappointed. Strangely enough, so did she. "Before I leave, I'd love if you would show me around. Are you still free to take me for a stroll tomorrow?" Suddenly, her heart pounded. Why did she say that? She'd already asked him earlier in the day and he'd agreed. Even to her own ears, she sounded overly eager—it was almost as though she was asking the preacher on a date. The words *it's not a date* were on her lips, but thankfully she held them back.

"That sounds wonderful," Molly said as she entered the room. "Joey is already asleep. Poor little guy was tired." She slid into the only empty chair, then turned to the preacher. "Would you like to say the prayer, Clyde? I understand if you'd rather not."

"Not at all," he answered, then reached for Faith and Molly's hands. Marcus completed the circle. "Lord, thank you for these wonderful people, and the food set out before us. Thank you too, for sending Faith to us. Please keep her safe on her journey home. Amen."

"Help yourselves," Molly said, and passed the platter of biscuits to the other end of the table for Clyde.

"They smell delicious, Molly, as your cooking always does. You definitely spoil me," Clyde said, and Faith knew his words came from the heart.

Molly chuckled. "Better than sausages, then?"

"I happen to like sausages," Clyde protested. "Just not every night."

Everyone laughed, including Clyde. The more she knew him, the more Faith liked the small town preacher.

Faith waited for Clyde to dish out his food, only it appeared he waited for the women to get theirs first. Just as he'd done at the diner. It surprised her when he reached for her plate and began to dish out her food. She wasn't used to being treated in this way, but it made her feel good. And definitely wanted.

"That's plenty, thank you, Clyde," she said, then took the plate from him.

"It's the least I can do," he said. "I'm sure you ladies have worked tirelessly on this excellent meal."

"It is mostly Molly's doing. She already had the stew going. I made the biscuits, which are simple." Faith glanced across at Molly. Marcus was dishing her food up. Did the men think women were incapable of helping themselves? The moment the thought entered her head, guilt filled Faith. She knew they meant no harm or disrespect. At least *these men* didn't.

She pushed the butter toward Clyde. "For the biscuits," she said, and he accepted the butter, then cut a biscuit in half. He then leaned forward and took in the aroma.

"I think I need a wife," he said, his voice full of laughter. "I could certainly take this every day."

Faith felt Molly's eyes on her, but she said nothing. For that, Faith was grateful. Her cousin had been trying to convince her to stay in Crystal Springs permanently, and she was sorely tempted. Except she had no way to support herself here.

Marcus had assured her it was unnecessary, that he was happy to support Molly's cousin. But that didn't sit well with Faith. She had always been an independent woman, and she vowed to continue that way. Marcus had even offered her a job as his receptionist. He was clutching at straws for her sake; she was certain. Until now, Marcus had managed on his own. Why would that change now?

Marcus joined in the laughter. "It's the best thing I've ever done," Marcus said. "Even if we did have a rocky start. And that was before we even married!" He reached for Molly's hand then, and Faith watched as the pair linked hands. Molly and Marcus had true love. It was something she longed for, but so far, real love had eluded her.

Clyde turned to her and smiled. Faith was certain he was thinking along the same lines. Not everyone found their one true love. Some were gifted with a second chance, but for many, love eluded them for their entire lives.

It was all part of God's plan. If He planned she should not marry, there had to be a reason for that.

Sometime later, they finished eating. "Thank you for a delicious meal," Clyde said as he wiped his lips with the cloth napkin. "I appreciate you convincing me to come along tonight." His eyes then turned to Faith and he smiled. "Wonderful food, and even better company."

"Let me get you some coffee," Molly said, then returned to the table with the coffeepot.

Faith stood too and cleared the table of the first course. She pulled the apple pie she'd made out of the oven. The aroma was amazing. No doubt the preacher would love it, too. The poor man seemed deprived of good food.

Surely there was a way to remedy that?

Chapter Five

Clyde was used to being invited for meals. That was nothing new.

What was new was the way he felt tonight. It was different, and he wasn't sure why. He'd dined with Molly and Marcus often before, and was right at home with them. Joey was growing up fast, and his personality was showing. They were a wonderful family, and one he adored.

The only change to all of this was… Faith. There was something about her that put him on edge.

No, that wasn't right. He wasn't on edge around her—it was a totally different feeling. Dennis Andrews at the mercantile put him on edge. Faith was the opposite. Her presence had him relaxing. His heart fluttered when she was close by, and warmth flooded him.

If it had been a parishioner explaining these feelings to him, Clyde knew exactly what he would tell them. Except now the shoe was on the other foot, and he had no intention of trying to analyze it. For him, it couldn't be true.

"Apple pie, Clyde?" Faith's voice cut through his musings. "Help yourself to cream." She placed a large slice of pie in front of him and pointed to the bowl of cream.

Their eyes met, and he was suddenly flustered. "Thank you," he said, trying to muster up a smile. If his reactions were what he thought they were, Clyde wanted no part of it. He was certain Faith would feel the same.

Wouldn't she?

Of course she would. She'd told him she was only staying for a matter of days, so there was no point in even contemplating…what? They could be friends, but nothing more than that. It suited them both perfectly. Didn't it?

He was second-guessing himself, and Clyde wanted no part of it. He was the town preacher, for goodness' sake. There was no rule that said he couldn't marry, but as a bachelor, he led an uncomplicated life. He preferred it that way.

"This is excellent pie. Thank you both for a magnificent meal." Clyde couldn't believe how truly delicious the pie was.

"It's all Faith's doing. She made the pie," Molly offered, then glanced across at her cousin, a smile tugging at her lips.

Clyde's heart pounded. Had Molly turned matchmaker now? He shook himself mentally. Surely not. It wasn't enough the townsfolk had to endure Dennis's antics in matching folks up, now Molly was doing it too?

He must be wrong. Molly wouldn't do that to him. Although Faith was her cousin…

Clyde reached for the mug of coffee sitting in front of him. Delicious. Molly was known for her amazing coffee when she worked at the bakery. It was far better than the coffee Joel had made before her arrival.

He licked his lips as he put the mug back on the table. It had been a wonderful evening, but perhaps he should leave now.

"Shall we move to the sitting room while the women clean up?" Marcus asked.

Without a word, Molly quickly refilled their mugs.

How could he refuse now? "Sounds good," he said without emotion, and Marcus frowned.

Taking their mugs of coffee, the men moved out of the kitchen, and out of earshot of the women. Clyde settled himself into one of the comfortable chairs, and Marcus sat nearby. "Is something wrong, Clyde? You seem on edge tonight." The other man knew him far too well.

"It's Faith," he whispered, leaning forward to ensure he wasn't overheard.

Marcus frowned at first, then grinned. "You like her," he said. It was a statement, not a question. "What is wrong with that?"

"I'm a preacher. Besides, she's leaving soon." Clyde's heart was pounding, and he wasn't certain why. He considered Marcus his best friend in all of Crystal Springs.

Marcus frowned again. "There is no rule that says preachers can't marry. We both know many do."

Clyde leaned back in his chair again. "She's leaving town in a few days," he said firmly.

"Perhaps," Marcus said, with no other explanation.

It was frustrating, but also piqued Clyde's interest. "Perhaps? What does that mean?" His heart pounding in his head, Clyde leaned forward again.

Marcus sighed. "It's not my story, so don't ask, but things are up in the air."

Did that mean Faith would stay longer? Permanently? Or was he reading far too much into Marcus's words? It was more likely the latter. Besides, it didn't affect Clyde either way.

"More coffee, Clyde?" Faith asked as she strolled into the sitting room.

His heart fluttered, but Clyde decided it was merely because he worried she might have overheard the conversation. "Thank you, but no. I'll never sleep tonight. Besides," he said firmly, "I've kept you good folk up late as it is."

"Not at all," Molly said, close on Faith's heels. "You are welcome to stay if you would like. Whatever works best for you."

Faith reached out to take his now empty mug, and their fingers brushed. A rush of heat ran up his arm, and he knew it was far better if he left. This was all his fault—he shouldn't have taken her to the diner. He'd gotten to know Faith better than expected, and found he really liked her. He wasn't sure how he felt, but the guarded glances between her and Molly gave him an inkling she did. "Thank you again for the meal, and for the wonderful company. I'm not one to retire late, so I will be away."

Faith appeared disappointed. "Are we still going on our stroll tomorrow?" she asked, her voice almost pleading.

Now he was torn. He'd pushed their arrangement to the back of his mind. Was it a good idea to spend even more time with her? Probably not, but he'd made an arrangement, and wouldn't go back on his word. "Of course," he said. "Shall I collect you at, say, ten?"

Face beaming, Faith answered, "Ten is perfect. I'll see you then." She walked him to the front door after all the goodbyes were over. When the door closed behind him, Clyde felt as though he'd left something behind.

Despite all his protests to the contrary, he knew it was Faith. He missed her already.

Chapter Six

"What about this gown?" Faith held yet another gown up in front of herself. She stared at her reflection.

Molly frowned. "You do know Clyde is taking you for a stroll around town, and nothing more, right? Besides, what is wrong with what you're wearing?" She put her hands on her hips. "You're leaving the day after tomorrow, so what is the point of all this?"

"I know, but I like him." She leaned in conspiratorially and whispered. "I think he likes me, too."

Molly's eyes opened wide in astonishment. "He does, I'm certain he does. The fact you're leaving town means you can't lead him on. Just because you're my cousin does not mean I'll stand back and allow you to play with Clyde's emotions." She pursed her lips then.

Faith dropped to the bed and sat with her shoulders slumped. "You're right. It's not fair." She shook her head then. "If I was staying permanently, things could be different. But I'm not." Faith put her hands to her face. "I'm a terrible person. We both know I am—what happened back home confirmed it."

Molly came to sit beside her. "That was not your fault, so please don't blame yourself." Molly pulled her cousin close and hugged her. "Are you even sure you want to go home?"

If she was truthful with herself, Faith knew she didn't want to leave. "I love it here in Crystal Springs, but I will not continue to impose on you and Marcus. Besides, I have no way to support myself, and therefore, it is impossible for me to stay."

She stood then and pulled yet another gown from the closet. "This one?" she asked, staring in the mirror once more.

There was a knock at the door.

"What you're wearing is perfect," Molly called as she left the room. "Clyde is here. Hurry."

The mere thought of the preacher had her heart fluttering. Faith was in a frenzy and got ready as quickly as she could. Molly was right though, she needed to make a decision. She either left Crystal Springs and returned home, or she stayed put. If she left, it meant she would likely never see Clyde again. If she did the latter, would he even care?

She had a dilemma that only Faith could resolve. For now, she needed to ready herself for their stroll around town.

Their stroll was nothing more than friends.

Faith hurried to the bathroom and freshened up. After splashing water on her face, she fixed her hair. There was nothing wrong with it except a few strands of hair had escaped. Molly was right—the gown she was wearing already was perfect for the occasion. Why did the thought of strolling around town with Clyde make her nervous? He made her the least anxious of anyone she knew.

She snatched up her reticule from her room before heading toward the sitting room, where Faith was certain she would find Molly and Clyde. Her belief confirmed, she stood in the doorway. "Good morning," she said as she put a fake smile on her face. "I apologize for keeping you waiting."

Clyde stood and stepped toward her. "Good morning," he said cheerfully. "You look beautiful." He paused momentarily, his eyes moving from her eyes to her feet. "Are you ready?"

Faith felt the heat travel up her neck to her cheeks and ducked her face to disguise her embarrassment. Clyde offered his arm, and Faith hooked her arm through his. "I am ready," Faith said, and the pair headed toward the front door.

"Crystal Springs is quite small," Clyde said once they were outside. "You probably worked that out already." He grinned then, and Faith couldn't help but smile. This time, there was nothing fake about it. "Have you had a chance to look about at all?"

"Not really," she answered. "I've been to the church, as you know. And the diner, as you also know. Oh, and I walked past the bakery." She laughed then, and he grinned again.

Clyde ran a hand over his beard-covered face. It made Faith wonder what he was thinking. "How do you feel about visiting the small park behind the stores? It's not far," he added.

"I'll be led by you. I know nothing about this town. Apart from my cousin and Marcus, and you, of course, I know no one." This time, she giggled. Why was she behaving like a teenage girl out on a first date? Faith did not know. Especially after what she'd endured at the hands of another man.

Suddenly, she pulled away from Clyde. The memory of that day flashed before her, and her heart pounded. Molly tried to warn her it was too soon, but Faith would have none of it. Besides, she was fine yesterday when he took her to the diner.

"Faith? Are you alright?" Clyde's voice was full of concern. He was leading her somewhere. Where she didn't know. It only increased her sense of panic. "I'm going to sit you on a wooden bench." His hands gripped her arms and Clyde assisted her onto the bench. Within moments, he was sitting next to her.

"I… I'm alright," she whispered, knowing full well she wasn't.

"Should I get Marcus? Or Molly?"

"No!" Faith was adamant about that. She had to move on. It was the only way forward.

Clyde reached for her hand. His hand was gentle, and she didn't pull away, which surprised Faith. She knew, though, Clyde would never hurt her. "What can I do to help?" he asked softly.

Closing her eyes, Faith leaned back onto the wooden bench. She shook her head. "I'll be fine. Just give me a minute. Please?" she begged, fighting back the tears that threatened to fall.

She wondered what Clyde thought of all this nonsense. It was likely enough to scare him away.

They sat together quietly, for goodness knew how long. Faith felt comforted by Clyde's presence, and he didn't ask questions. He continued to hold her hand, and for that, she was grateful. Certain Clyde was used to this sort of thing—sitting with a distraught parishioner—he was likely more patient than most people would be.

Finally, her heart calmed, and her lightheadedness dissipated. Faith opened her eyes and turned to Clyde. "I am very sorry. I believe I'm ready to continue."

He didn't loosen his gentle hold on her hand. Instead, he gave it a gentle squeeze. "Only if you're sure. I don't mind sitting here with you for as long as necessary. Quiet contemplation is good for the soul."

Clyde was right. Quiet contemplation was good for the soul. She needed to remember that. Perhaps the next time she had a panic attack, heaven forbid there was a next time, she needed to do just that. She smiled cautiously, then stood. Clyde stood with her, his hand still clasping hers.

"Do you want to return home?" He didn't seem upset at the prospect, but Faith was having none of it.

"Not at all. I'm fine now." She licked her lips. "I…" Faith didn't want to explain, but she owed Clyde an explanation.

He put a hand up to halt her words. "You don't have to tell me anything unless you want to. There is certainly no obligation." He turned them toward the park, and they were soon on their way. The pair walked there in silence, and for the first time in a long time, Faith felt at peace. Whether it was the peacefulness of Crystal Springs or the company she was in, Faith didn't know. But she liked it.

"Well, this is it," Clyde said, spreading his hands wide. "It's small, but I often come here for that quiet contemplation I mentioned earlier. Some call it meditation—whatever you prefer."

There was a small pergola in the middle of the park, surrounded by a variety of flowers and low bushes. Birds twittered, and the sun was shining. Faith could ask for nothing more.

He indicated for her to sit on a seat in the pergola, and she did. When Clyde sat next to her, Faith sidled up beside him. His presence was more than a little comforting, and in some ways that worried Faith. It was surely a good thing?

"When are you leaving?" he asked quietly, his voice unsure. He didn't seem happy about the prospect, but neither was she. Why was she even contemplating returning home? There was nothing there to entice her back, and the place was full of difficult memories.

She turned to face him. "I haven't decided. If I return, it will be soon."

His head shot up. "If you return? Is there some question about that?" He seemed more than a little surprised, which was not hard to understand. Her statement had surprised even Faith.

"Something happened in Violet Town, and I…" She licked her lips again, then glanced up at him. Clyde reached for her hand again, but didn't interrupt. It was as though he understood without being told. A tear rolled down her face, and he wiped it away.

What happened next surprised Faith, but she didn't protest.

Chapter Seven

It was clear to Clyde something was terribly wrong. Something devastating had happened to Faith, and it had left her traumatized. The fact she couldn't bring herself to return to her hometown was very telling.

Without giving it a thought, he pulled her into his arms.

Faith didn't protest, and she rested her head against his shoulder. Her tears flowed, but she said not a word. He wouldn't press her for an explanation. That wasn't helpful. Of their own volition, his hands worked in circles over her back. He prayed it was comforting to her.

From experience, Clyde knew it wasn't always words that gave comfort to people. Sometimes, just being there during the difficult moments was what mattered. This seemed to be one of those times. He was pleased he'd brought her here—*the garden of peace* Clyde called it, and often recommended members of his flock come here when their minds were in turmoil. It was the perfect setting to see and feel the extent of God's gifts.

After a while, Faith lifted her head. Tears streaked her face, and he wiped them away, then pulled a handkerchief from his pocket and handed it to her. Red blotted her cheeks—he had no doubt she felt embarrassed. There was no need. Emotions needed to be acknowledged, otherwise they were bottled up and nothing good came of it.

He looked at her and smiled. "Feeling better?"

She nodded her head, then rested it on his shoulder again. Clyde wasn't sure he ever wanted to let her go. "Take what I say with a grain of salt, but did you perhaps think if you're having doubts, there might be a reason?"

Faith stared at him, her eyes not leaving his. She licked her lips again. An action he now realized was born of anxiety. "Molly said the same thing." Her eyes suddenly went to her hands as she twisted them in her lap.

"It is clear you are traumatized. In my opinion, take it or leave it, you need to heal. Can that be achieved if you return to Violet Town?" He brushed a strand of hair back behind her ear. "Only you can make that decision, and it won't be an easy one."

She lifted her eyes to study him. The expression that crossed her face was one of acknowledgement. Had no one asked that question before? Then again, he was far more experienced in this area than most others in town. Even Marcus. The fact the doctor sent patients to the preacher for counseling from time to time proved that point.

Faith stared at him a little longer, then suddenly her face softened. Had she decided already?

"You're right," she said firmly. "Going back will achieve nothing. I need to stay here in Crystal Springs. Marcus and Molly have already said they're willing to have me for as long as I want to stay. I'd be a fool to refuse their offer."

He was trying not to be selfish about the situation. Of course, he wanted her to stay, but for his own reasons, and that shouldn't have even entered his mind. "If you're interested, I can help with the healing." She stared at him, but didn't say a word. "It would involve counseling sessions at least every other day."

She frowned. "You've done this before?"

Clyde totally understood her reluctance. "Many times. It's your choice, and there is no obligation. Oh, and there is no cost involved—it's all part of the service I provide."

Faith seemed to mull over her decision. It would be different if he was a complete stranger, Clyde was certain. In many ways, he was, but they seemed to have become close rather quickly. It was surprising, especially to him. He'd always been a loner—it went with the job. He'd kept people at a distance, and it suited him fine.

Faith was different. Whether that was because she needed his help, Clyde wasn't sure. He suspected it went far deeper than that. At this point, he wasn't prepared to try and analyze what that might be.

"How would that work?" she suddenly asked, her voice barely above a whisper. "Do I have to tell Molly?"

Her expression was one of utter sadness. Clyde wanted to change that. "You don't have to tell anyone. We can take a stroll each time if you prefer. You set the rules."

She sighed. "Can we come here for those sessions? It brings me peace—of sorts."

He smiled then. It was a special place—he'd learned that long ago. Clyde was pleased Faith had recognized it for what it was. A spiritual place where those who visited were filled with hope. "We certainly can. Would you like to stay here a little longer? I thought a visit to the diner would be in order, but perhaps you'd rather not."

Faith shook her head. "I'm a mess," she said. "Do you mind if we stay here instead?"

He didn't mind at all. His arm went up around her shoulders, and Faith leaned into him. Clyde could stay like this all day, but knew he shouldn't. If he was to counsel her, did that make her a client, or could he do it as a friend? Now he was torn. And because of confidentiality, he couldn't seek advice. He would have to ponder, but knew he'd already crossed the line of Faith being considered a client.

And frankly, he didn't care.

Clyde left Faith at the park for a short time and went to the bakery. He brought four mixed cakes, then returned to the park. Sitting there in the fresh air was invigorating. Sitting next to Faith was heart-warming.

He didn't know how long it would take for her to heal, and when she asked, he spoke the truth. "It's a long process. It could be weeks or months. For some, healing takes far longer." She nodded briefly and went back to eating. "You've acknowledged your pain, and that's the first step," he said. That seemed to appease her, and a small smile tugged at her lips.

Warmth filled him. Clyde desperately wanted to help Faith. It was his job, he knew that, but more than that he was her friend, even if they'd only known each other for a short time.

They finished eating, and he suggested a stroll through the park. The seats here were hard, and after a while, a person could feel quite stiff. He stood, then helped Faith to her feet. Not that she needed help, but he enjoyed it when they touched. He liked having her near. "These gardens are reasonably large," he told her. "This path circles around the pergola, and is surrounded by trees and flowers." Her questioning look had him explaining further. "The Ladies Auxiliary maintains the gardens, along with any of the townsfolk who feel so inclined. It's a wonderful place for people to simply come and sit, or for their children to play while the parents reflect."

"I couldn't agree more," Faith said. "I'd bring my children here if I had any." Suddenly she brought her hands to her mouth, and her expression changed. In a matter of moments, she went from relative happiness to what appeared to be terror. Or something close to it.

He reached out and touched her shoulder. The movement startled her, and she jumped. "Everything is alright, Faith," he whispered. "You're safe here."

As if coming out of a trance, her eyes opened wide, and she stared into his face. She nodded, then briefly closed her eyes. "I know," she whispered, then continued walking as if nothing had occurred.

As they ambled around the perimeter of the gardens, Faith squatted down now and then to smell the flowers. They had a beautiful aroma, both collectively and individually. This was a place Clyde enjoyed visiting in pleasant weather. In the winter, he rarely came, as it was far too cold. When the sun shone, it was great. The fresh air, and being surrounded by God's natural gifts, always lifted him up. It helped his clients too.

Clyde felt sure it would be the right place for him to bring Faith. It had already seemed to help. "It truly is lovely here," Faith said. "I am looking forward to coming here with you." He couldn't help but smile. His mind was sending him a warning signal, but his heart was ready to accept.

Never before had he felt this way about a woman, but there was still the possibility Faith would leave. Her leaving would be delayed because of his counseling, but as far as he could tell, she still planned to go back to Violet Town where her trauma had apparently occurred. His heart thudded.

He knew from the moment they met she was only here short term, but he didn't know her then. Not really. Since then, they'd spent many hours together. He wanted to spend many more. Clyde knew in his heart it was a bad idea. He was already feeling connected to Faith. But she needed his help, and he had no intention of letting her down. There was no one else in town qualified.

No, he needed to do this. He just had to ensure he guarded his heart along the way.

Chapter Eight

Faith breathed in the fragrance of the countless flowers they encountered along the way. She couldn't thank Clyde enough for bringing her here. It was strange neither Molly nor Marcus mentioned it. Then again, they likely didn't want her to come here alone.

After what had happened, Faith totally understood.

She glanced about. This place, beautiful as it was, sat secluded from town. It was behind the main street, out of view. And wasn't that part of the reason things went down the way they did back home? The thought made her shudder.

Clyde put a hand to her shoulder. It was as though he could read her thoughts. His touch was comforting, and she didn't want to leave his presence. Not ever. Of course, that was impossible. He had work to do—she wasn't his priority, so they would have to part ways at some point today. That thought made her feel hollow. It was not something Faith had experienced before. She didn't know how to process it.

She could ask Molly, but then she'd have to explain why she was staying longer. Faith didn't have the strength to do that. Not yet anyway. She would tell Molly and Marcus when she felt ready to do so. Neither would hold it against her, she was certain. She was lucky to have them. They restored her faith in humanity, just as Clyde had done.

She glanced across at the preacher and smiled. Peace had overtaken her soon after they'd arrived. Faith totally understood why he came here, and why he brought people here for sessions.

"You're allowed to pick the flowers—if that's what you'd like to do," Clyde said, his voice pulling her out of her wayward thoughts. "The gardens are maintained to bring people pleasure." He smiled then, and Faith's heart thudded.

"They truly are beautiful," she said, looking up at him. "But I don't have the heart to do it. I'd rather leave them here for others to enjoy, too."

Clyde reached out a hand to help her to her feet. A zing of…she had no idea what, ran up her arm. The more time she spent with the preacher, the more enamored she became. They were two of a kind, she and Clyde. Both loners, and both lonely. Only she lived with demons, and he was the demon slayer. At least that's what he told her, but not in so many words.

She could easily picture Clyde helping people through the worst time of their lives. He was soft-spoken, and he listened carefully to every word. His eyes didn't miss anything either. She didn't feel watched, but she knew he took in her every movement. But not in a sinister way.

The truth was, Clyde made her feel safe and seen. Few people did that for her. Of course, Marcus and Molly did, but they were family. She adored them and their baby boy. If she could stay in Crystal Springs forever, that's exactly what Faith would do. The town was small, and everyone so far had been friendly.

It always came back to finding employment. Her heart sank. It wasn't a town with many opportunities to earn a living. Of course, Marcus had offered her a job, but in truth, he didn't need her. His offer was only because she was family. Nothing more. And Faith wasn't one to want to marry, to have someone support her, as many women did. It simply wasn't in her nature.

She hooked her arm through Clyde's and they continued their walk through the fragrant and peaceful gardens. She fully understood why he called this place the *gardens of peace*.

Neither of them spoke again until they came to the end of the garden path. "Shall I walk you back home now, or is there somewhere else you'd like to go?"

Faith felt more relaxed after their time at the gardens.

"I'd rather stay here all day, but we both know that can't happen."

Clyde leaned forward and tucked some stray hair behind her ear. "No, unfortunately, but shall we reconvene tomorrow?" Clyde studied her. "I can collect you from home around the same time if you'd like. We'll come here again, and talk."

Faith was confused. "Talk?"

A small smile tugged at Clyde's lips. "Talk is what most people do in those sessions we discussed."

"Oh." Faith knew that already, but it hadn't really sunk in. Of course, she would have to tell Clyde what happened. How else could he help her? Heat flowed up to her cheeks, and she turned her head away.

"There's nothing to be embarrassed about," he said, the moment she felt the heat in her face. "It is how you heal."

Faith nodded. She already knew that to be true, but voicing the most difficult time in her life would not be easy. Not for her to speak the words, or even for him to hear them. "Can we take the longest route home?" she asked, not wanting to leave his side as yet.

Clyde chuckled. "We certainly can."

He turned them in a different direction, and Faith was glad to stall her arrival back home. Or, more truthfully, to spend more time with the preacher she'd come to know, care for, and respect.

"Did you have a pleasant walk?" Molly asked as Faith entered the kitchen. Little Joey was on the floor banging pans together.

"I did," Faith said, sitting at the kitchen table as Molly placed a mug of tea there for her. "Clyde is…" she almost let slip their plans. "He's going to collect me again tomorrow. We spent a lot of time in the gardens." She took a mouthful of the hot beverage. "Molly, it's so beautiful there. Why didn't you tell me about that place?" She raised her eyebrows then, hoping her cousin would tell her the truth.

"I…I thought it would be too dangerous if you went alone. Lone women are vulnerable, as you know. Even in a place like Crystal Springs." Molly sighed then. "I'm sorry. It wasn't my decision to make." She smiled tentatively then. "At least Clyde took you there. I gather you stayed a long time."

Faith's heart filled with joy at the memory. "We did. Clyde called it the gardens of peace. It truly was— for me at least."

"I'm glad. Clyde is a good man. I'm pleased the two of you have connected." Molly seemed a little too enthusiastic for Faith's liking.

"You know him well?" She knew Marcus and Clyde were friends and should have realized Molly would know him equally well.

"Of course. He and Marcus spend time together. We often have him over for a meal as well." Just then, Joey slammed two pots together and the sound reverberated through Faith's ears. "Joey, no," Molly said firmly, taking the offending pots from the small boy's hands. Within moments, he scowled, then cried as though in agony. Which clearly he was not.

It was all Faith could do not to laugh. The boy's antics were funny, but it would never do to let him see her mirth. Molly reached into his toy box that sat in a corner of the kitchen. "Look, Joey. See what Mama has found!" Swinging a stuffed toy in front of his eyes, Joey was completely distracted from the pots and pans. Molly collected them up while he was preoccupied with the introduction of a different toy.

Faith studied the pair. What she wouldn't give to have a little family of her own. After what occurred, she knew it would never happen. How could she come back from that? What man would even have her? If she hadn't left the town of her own accord, she surely would have been banished. Or at the very least, ridiculed. Molly took her in at her time of need and was there to listen if she needed someone to open up to.

She had already made arrangements with Clyde for tomorrow. Otherwise, Faith knew she would back out. It wasn't something she was looking forward to—not the talking part, anyway. Spending time with Clyde was pure bliss.

Telling him her vile secret was another thing altogether.

 Chapter Nine

It was a new day, and hopefully a day of blessings for Faith. Clyde fidgeted about as he waited for the time to collect her.

Yesterday, he felt, was a good start. Not that she'd opened up to him at all, but today he had high hopes. He drank down the last of his coffee. Not only was it cold, it tasted dreadful. Molly made the best coffee—he wondered if she would teach Faith her *secret recipe*?

Clyde shook himself. If he went by Faith's own words, she wouldn't be here long enough for that to happen. His heart thudded. Why did he even care? Never before had he experienced these feelings. But never had he met someone quite like her.

It was clear Faith was troubled, but he intended to help banish her worries. His biggest concern was she wouldn't talk to him. For this to work, she had to discuss whatever had happened, as difficult as it might be.

Clyde rinsed his cup, then left the parsonage. Instead of a skip in his step, he felt as though he was walking toward doom. Would today cause a rift between them, or would a weight be lifted from her shoulders? He certainly hoped it would be the latter.

Approaching the house, he saw a curtain pull back slightly. Did that mean Faith was excited to see him, or was she dreading his arrival? He wanted to assume she was excited. Or at the very least, happy he was there.

Clyde shook himself mentally. This was all about Faith. None of what they would undertake would benefit him.

"Good morning," he told Faith as she opened the front door. He didn't even get the chance to knock. She smiled, and his heart fluttered.

Since when did a woman's smile make his heart sing? Perhaps he wasn't the right person to do this. But if not him, then who? Not Marcus, since he was Molly's husband, and therefore, they were family. He had to accept there was no one else in town who could help Faith through this.

Clyde pulled back his shoulders, determined to assist Faith in overcoming her fears.

Suddenly, she shoved a paper bag toward him. "Molly made a snack for us," she said, her lips curling up again. "She insisted," Faith whispered.

How could he refuse? Besides, Molly was an excellent cook. It was sure to be delicious, whatever was in that bag.

"It's your favorite, blueberry muffins," Faith said, and he couldn't help but smile. Molly knew him far too well.

Paper bag in one hand, he offered his other arm. Warmth flooded him when Faith hooked her arm through his. Their closeness filled his heart with joy, but Clyde knew he should put those thoughts out of his mind.

"I didn't tell her," Faith said quietly as they headed toward the park. "Or Marcus."

He turned to face her. "It is your choice, Faith. It's between us until you decide otherwise. If you make that decision at all."

A tentative smile crossed her lips as they arrived at the pergola. The fragrance of the various flowers seemed to be already calming her. Faith sat down and waited for Clyde to join her. "Do you want the muffins now, or later?" he asked, putting the paper bag to one side.

"I think now. I...we might not feel like them later." Was she so convinced he would be upset about what she told him? Clyde had heard many scenarios over the years. It was doubtful he could be shocked at anything Faith told him.

He handed her the bag and Faith took a muffin from the bag, then offered the other one to Clyde. "They smell delicious," he said, breathing in the enticing aroma. "I don't know how Marcus isn't overweight."

His comment had Faith laughing. "It is a concern," she said, putting a hand to her belly. Then she tucked into the muffin. "Oh, they are delicious," Faith said, nibbling on the food in her hands.

Clyde pulled a chunk off his muffin. "I'm jealous of Marcus. Not that it's new," he said, laughing. "I've told him on many occasions." His eyes studied her. Clyde wondered if eating the muffins now was Faith's way of putting off the inevitable.

They sat in silence as they each ate their blueberry muffin. Clyde made a mental note to thank Molly when they returned. Soon, they had both finished eating. His hands were quite sticky, and it seemed Faith's were too. "Would you like to clean your hands?" he asked. "There's a stream not far away."

Faith glanced down at her hands. "That's probably a good idea," she said, and Clyde helped her to her feet. He shoved the paper bag into his pocket, and would dispose of it later.

"It's just over there. Follow me." The stream was not far, and he led the way. Faith's eyes opened wide in surprise when they arrived. The crystal clear water was good enough to drink, and many of the townsfolk did exactly that. A short way upstream were a few ducks. She seemed surprised, but said nothing.

Faith's eyes seemed to follow the path of the stream, up toward the hills. "Is this how the town got its name?" she asked, curiosity filling her voice.

"It is. The springs are miles away, though. You can't see them from here. Perhaps one day I'll take you there." The moment he made the offer, Clyde realized he'd made a promise he may not be able to keep. If Faith left town, as she likely would, the opportunity would disappear.

Faith studied him. "I'd like that." They both cleaned their hands in the clear water, then Faith cupped her hands and tasted the water. "This is perfect," she said, surprise on her face.

Although he'd done it many times before, Clyde scooped up some of the water and drank it. It was cold and untarnished. The townsfolk often collected water here, but they respected the fact they needed to preserve it for future generations, too.

"Are you ready?" Clyde asked, and Faith immediately seemed to know what he was talking about. She nodded her head. "Do you want to sit or walk?" Many people found it easier to open up while soaking up the surrounding beauty.

"I'd like to walk, if you don't mind." Faith's eyes met his, but only momentarily. She hooked her arm through Clyde's and they began their journey.

Faith took a deep breath, then let it out slowly. Clyde knew she would have been dreading this moment. She even told him she hadn't slept well worrying about it. "I don't know where to start," she whispered, and Clyde squeezed her hand.

"At the beginning. That's where your troubles began, right?"

She nodded her head. "I met Lucius in my last years at school. We're around the same age, and his family moved to Violet Town a few months earlier. He was nice, attentive." She stopped walking and stared down at the ground. Clyde didn't push her. This was a process she had to lead. He did little talking during these sessions, and mostly listened. "One day, he kissed me at the back of the school shed." She glanced up at him momentarily, then sighed.

She searched for his hand, then gripped it, as though he were her lifeline. "I pushed him away," Faith said, her eyes searching his. He wasn't here to judge and said nothing. "He simply came back at me. I was thirteen and confused." Faith stopped walking and closed her eyes. Clyde stopped too. He glanced about, but there were no benches nearby. Perhaps that was a good thing.

Faith took a few steps before she began again. "He left school not long after that, and I saw little of him." Faith told Clyde she'd kept her distance after her last encounter with Lucius, and all seemed well. Until it wasn't.

"I recently bumped into him in town. To be honest," she said, turning to face him, "I thought he'd left town. It had been years since I'd seen him." A shudder went through her, and Clyde knew she was replaying those moments in her mind. "One moment I was on the boardwalk minding my own business after shopping, and the next…" She took a long breath and let it out slowly.

Clyde put a hand to her back to assure Faith he was still there, and she was safe. "The next I was being dragged into an alleyway. If it hadn't been for my shopping strewn across the boardwalk, it could have been worse."

Tears filled her eyes, but Faith fought them back. Clyde hoped she would let her emotions go, as she would feel far better if she did.

They had reached one of the wooden benches along the way, and he motioned toward it, not wanting to break the spell. Faith nodded, and they sat. How long they would stay there remained to be seen.

"He…" She closed her eyes again. "He tore off my clothes, and if the sheriff hadn't investigated why there were groceries everywhere, I know it would have been worse." This time, tears ran slowly down her face. Clyde's fingers itched to wipe them away, but he couldn't. He had to let her continue. "The sheriff dragged Lucius to jail, then returned with a blanket for me." She turned to Clyde then. "I couldn't leave the alleyway in that state of undress." He nodded. It was the first time he had interrupted her commentary.

Faith wiped at her tears and sat back. Clearly not prepared to say anything else.

"Where is he now?" Clyde asked.

Turning to look at him, Faith brushed back a tendril of hair. "As far as I'm aware, he's still in jail." She glanced down at her hands, twisting in her lap.

"None of it is your fault. You understand that, don't you?"

Faith's head shot up. "There must be a reason he targeted me. Otherwise, it wouldn't have happened."

The mindset of victims—it was the biggest hurdle to jump. Clyde reached for her hand again. "He targeted you because you're a good person. This Lucius, that evil man, believed he could get away with it. None of it was your fault. Please remember that."

This time, the tears flowed heavily. No more holding back. It was exactly what Clyde wanted to see. Suddenly, Faith flew into his arms. As much as Clyde knew he shouldn't, he wrapped his arms around her, and comforted Faith the best way he knew how—he held her tight and didn't let go until her tears subsided.

It was at that very moment Clyde knew something in their relationship had shifted. He'd been afraid of it before they began, but he wouldn't fight it. He was certain they were meant to be together. His faith was a huge part of his life, and now he was certain this was fate.

God had a plan for everyone, and Clyde was certain His plan was only now coming to fruition.

Chapter Ten

Faith felt wretched. She was exhausted, despite doing virtually nothing. She was pleased Clyde had brought her to the gardens of peace. It helped immensely.

His gentle and kind words had made an enormous difference. Molly had told her virtually the same things Clyde had, but she was family—of course she would say that. "Can we stay here a little longer?" she asked as they stood again. The greenery surrounding them filled Faith with a sense of belonging, as well as peacefulness.

She wasn't sure if confessing to Clyde had caused it, or whether it was her beautiful surroundings. Either way, she couldn't wish to be anywhere else right now.

"Whatever you want," Clyde said. He didn't show any emotion when she'd told him the awful details of her encounters with Lucius. There was no expression of shock, nor did he show disgust toward her. If his words were true, it wasn't Faith who was to blame, but Lucius.

Why, then, had Faith blamed herself for this occurrence? Was it as Clyde said, that she was a victim of an evil man? "Thank you," she said, turning to face him. "For everything."

Clyde smiled. It set her heart fluttering. "I didn't do much. I merely listened. Understand, though, this won't be the end of your pain."

She felt shocked. Not the end? "I thought…"

Clyde shook his head. "It can take some time. We discussed this yesterday, if you recall."

Now that he mentioned it, she did recall that conversation. "You're right. I remember now." Her voice sounded defeated, even to Faith. "Perhaps we should do this again?"

For what seemed minutes but was mere seconds, Clyde studied her. "It is totally your call. Sometimes just walking through these gardens with someone who understands can have healing powers."

It was Faith's turn to smile. She could understand that. This place, this *garden of peace*, as Clyde called it, had already helped her a lot. She felt more at ease now than she had since… She let the thought fade. Faith didn't want to think about that day.

"Shall we reconvene tomorrow?" Clyde asked, pulling her out of her thoughts. "Or in two days? Your choice."

Faith stared at him. It took a moment to understand the question. Her mind was in a state of confusion, and she wasn't sure why. As though he understood, Clyde guided her back to a sitting position. "It's not unusual," he said gently. "This confusion after the first session. Shall we sit for a while?"

Faith nodded. Why was she so confused? She knew what had happened, and who had done it.

"It's the realization of what was done to you," he whispered. "It's the reason I suggested we reconvene tomorrow. That way, you can get it sorted in your own mind."

Clyde reached for her hand and held it loosely. Faith reveled in his touch. She was more confused than ever. Did she like him touching her for comfort or another reason completely? She'd already decided having feelings for a preacher was a sin, and now she had confirmed it with herself. Clyde was only interested in her as a parishioner. Someone he could help through her worries.

She would meet with him tomorrow and then return home to Violet Town. Except she didn't want to go back—she had been attacked and humiliated. Not to mention made to feel ashamed of *her* actions. Not that Faith had done anything to be ashamed about. She wasn't the one who dragged another person into a dark alleyway and tried to…

Gasping for air, she quickly stood. Her head spun, but gentle hands gripped her arms and stopped her from falling.

"Faith." The words echoed in her head, and she felt herself being pulled down to the wooden bench again. "You are safe here with me, Faith." This time, his words were clear and comforting.

She nodded, trying to show him she understood. Hot tears ran down her cheeks. When did that happen? She swiped at them, trying to hide the fact. Clyde put an arm around her, and she sank into him.

Today had been harder than she'd imagined. Faith knew it would be difficult, but telling Clyde her story had brought up even more memories than she'd anticipated. How long would another person's actions affect her? When would she be able to move forward with her life?

Clyde handed her a handkerchief, and she wiped her eyes. "I'm sorry," she said before handing it back.

"Don't apologize," he said quietly. "This is all part of the healing process. It's doing you good."

Good? It didn't feel that way right now. Her heart was hammering, and her head pounding. Faith felt wretched, but she didn't want to leave here. She certainly didn't want Clyde to leave her side.

Suddenly she heard the twitter of birds, and the water running in the stream. Why hadn't she heard them before? Had they only begun now? She stood and glanced about. High in the trees, Cardinals sat and sang their little hearts out. She spotted some Robins up there too.

Faith heard the scamper of tiny feet. Squirrels and mice ran across in front of her. She ambled across to the stream. Several small turtles swam upstream in the clear water, a variety of fish nearby. She now understood why Clyde had brought her here, to this special place. It was filled with God's creatures. Lifting her heart of her burdens had helped her to see the true beauty of these gardens.

Faith didn't want to leave here—not today, not ever. How did she stay here in Crystal Springs, though? Clyde was in her heart, but for him, she was just another person who needed his help.

Suddenly, her heart shattered. In that moment, Faith knew she had to leave. The sooner the better, otherwise she would never recover from the heartache, and where would she be then?

Walking beside the preacher as he walked her home some time later, Faith thought long and hard about her future. She wouldn't go back to Violet Town. That was despite realizing what happened was not her fault. Not even slightly. Now she was torn about where she should go to once she left Crystal Springs.

She hadn't discussed it with Clyde, although she was certain he would try to talk her out of it. Nothing she did caused Lucius to attack her. Luck had been on her side when the sheriff happened past and noticed her scattered groceries.

Faith stumbled at the thought, and Clyde steadied her. Their eyes met, and she was frozen, couldn't pull her eyes away. He was the one to make a move, his eyes looking down at the ground. "There is a bit of a dip here," he said, not contemplating any other cause. Faith had no doubt Clyde knew exactly what caused her to trip, and it wasn't a non-existent dip on the path.

"Thank you," she said quietly, needing to acknowledge his help.

His hands suddenly fell from her, and his lips curled, but only momentarily. It was as though he knew their time together was short-lived. "I'm sure those long gowns women wear are not helpful in these circumstances." This time, his smile went all the way to his eyes.

Faith's heart thudded. The pair were growing closer by the day. In some ways, she wished Clyde had not offered to help her through her anxiety. In other ways, she was glad he did. Already her burdens were lessened, and that was his doing. "Shall we reconvene tomorrow?" He stared into her face as they approached the house. Faith didn't answer immediately, and he frowned. "I understand if it's too much. Take tomorrow to rest."

She closed her eyes and took a deep breath. Faith felt pulled in all directions. Clyde had been incredibly good to her. He had befriended her when she felt completely alone. And he helped her through a difficult time. Clyde was still helping her. "I haven't told Molly or Marcus yet," she almost whispered, although they were completely alone. "It feels as though I am deceiving them." She licked her lips, as they felt incredibly dry, but Faith knew it was the stress of her situation. Marcus had told her so, and since he was a doctor, she had to believe him.

Clyde's eyes followed her every move, just as she followed his. They were attuned to each other, there was no doubt. The revelation made Faith even more determined to leave town. Wasn't there a rule that preachers couldn't marry? Not that she wanted to marry Clyde. No, that wasn't even something she would contemplate.

"Thank you for your help today, Clyde," Faith said when they arrived back home. "I believe I shall rest tomorrow, if that's alright with you."

She watched his reaction, but Clyde didn't frown, and didn't seem surprised. "It's perfectly fine. If you change your mind, call into the church. I have nothing pressing I need to do." He reached out and took her hand, squeezing it gently, then walked away. Faith watched him until she could barely make out it was him. Then she hurried inside, leaning against the closed door, her breathing heavy.

"Whatever is wrong?" Molly asked as she headed Faith's way.

Faith took a fortifying breath and studied her cousin. "I have to leave town," she whispered. "I think I'm falling in love with the preacher."

It had been more than a week since Clyde began working with Faith. As they sat in the garden of peace, finishing the snacks Molly sent along with Faith, he pondered his situation. With every day that passed, Clyde felt even more drawn to her.

Faith had become far more than a client. He was falling in love with her. The problem was two-fold—he was working with her, and he was effectively her preacher. That surely meant he was breaking rules. The last thing he wanted was to place Faith in an unenviable position.

Not that she'd told him any such thing, or even indicated it was the case. If he was honest with himself, Clyde had seen a vast improvement in her. She didn't say a lot these days, but shared bits of information here and there. He never pushed her to open up—that's not the way it worked. When the person wanted to talk, they would. His job was to listen. Not interrupt, and not comment unless his opinion was sought.

"Do you want to leave, or would you prefer to stay a little longer?" Clyde asked, happy either way.

Faith studied him before speaking. "We should probably go," she said with a sigh. "There's always something I can do to help Molly." She smiled then and Clyde thought some happy memory had slipped into her mind.

He stood, then helped Faith to her feet. As she stepped forward, Faith lost her balance, and Clyde reached for her. He pulled her close against himself to steady her, then stared down into her face. Faith had voiced her wish to leave town soon. When Faith felt she was healed.

She would never be fully healed, but he couldn't tell her that. Nor did he want her to leave.

Without thinking, his arms went up around her, and he enveloped Faith, praying she never left. Her head rested against his chest, and Clyde was sure she felt the same way he did. What they should do about it, he wasn't sure. He was in an unenviable situation— he could be seen as using his position to begin a relationship. Only he'd been careful not to let that happen.

Until now.

He glanced down into her face, and Faith stared up at him. Clyde stared at her lips, then closed his eyes against the temptation. He couldn't do this. They couldn't do this—it went against everything he believed in.

Without warning, Faith's lips covered his. Somewhere, amongst his shock, was a need greater than he'd imagined he would ever possess. His arms tightened around her, and he heard Faith groan. It was enough to make Clyde come to his senses.

He stepped back. "We can't do this," he said, his voice husky. It was a sure sign things had gone too far.

She stared at him with her big blue eyes, then licked her lips. "We are both adults," she said firmly, and Clyde nodded his agreement.

"Except we are working together. Others may believe I coerced you." Clyde knew it to be true. The gossips in the town could, and would, twist anything to suit themselves. Even the most innocent scenarios.

Faith frowned then. "I don't care what people think anymore," she said. "Thanks to you. We have a right to be with whomever we choose to love."

Clyde stared at her in shock. "Love? Are you..." He had no clue Faith was in love with him. All this time they'd worked together, and she'd not said a word.

"Sure? I'm positive. I told Molly days ago, but we both believed it was better if I kept it to myself. Especially given you were helping me."

He supposed Molly was right to counsel Faith that way. If she'd asked him about another couple in a similar situation, he would have said the same thing. "I don't know where that leaves us," Clyde said as he stared down into her face. "Probably right back where we were before."

Faith didn't answer, but leaned her head against his chest once more. Clyde's arms circled her, and he sighed at the dilemma they found themselves in. Some of the townsfolk, Dennis, for instance, had assumed they were stepping out. It wasn't his place to say he was counseling Faith and didn't correct them.

Some days, it had felt like they were stepping out together. He always looked forward to collecting her and spending time together at the gardens. Watching the squirrels play and the rabbits hop away filled his heart. On each subsequent day, he saw the joy coming back into Faith's heart. She was a different person now from the unhappy woman he'd met that very first day.

Faith was suddenly up on her toes, her lips covering his again. "I love you, Clyde. I don't know how, but we need to work it out."

Clyde knew she was right, but did not know how they could fix it so the pair could be together.

After dropping her home, he took his time going back to the parsonage. He could feel Faith's anxiety with every step they took toward the Ryan home. Clyde felt certain she was on the verge of running, but doubted she would return to Violet Town. Not yet anyway. She felt humiliated there, although there was no reason to be. She had done nothing wrong.

He wanted to tell her straight out not to leave. But how could he do that? As a preacher, it was his duty to help heal people, not try to convince them to stay somewhere they didn't want to be. Clyde knew he was being selfish, but he didn't want to see her go. Still, he would accept whatever decision she made.

The closer he got to home, the more he felt the pull to enter the church and pray. The gardens might be a place of peace, but the church was far more important to him. All his adult life, Clyde had been a preacher. From a very young age, he knew his calling was to serve God. That didn't mean he wasn't permitted to fall in love. There was no such rule that forbid him from marrying.

Perhaps he should consult the archbishop about his dilemma. That entailed leaving town early in the morning and not returning until late that evening.

As he sat in the otherwise silent church, Clyde prayed for the strength to see Faith through her situation. He also prayed for the wisdom to know how to proceed. She was still quite fragile, and he had no intention of making matters worse for her.

He sat with his head in his hands and continued to pray. A sound at the entrance to the church pulled him out of his reflections. Clyde stood, turning to face where the noise had come from. His heart thudded as Faith entered the church. "Faith! I didn't expect to see you here." She was the last person he expected to see, since they'd not long parted. Not that he was complaining. His heart was filled with joy whenever she was near.

Clyde held out his hands to lead her into the church. Faith pulled her hands away, then suddenly offered them to him. He couldn't help but frown. "Is everything alright, Faith?" he asked, concerned their earlier conversation had upset her. Perhaps she was having second thoughts.

Faith shook her head vigorously. "Not really," she whispered.

Clyde glanced about. As far as he was aware, no one else was here. He saw no need for her to lower her voice like that. "You can tell me," he said, trying to keep the concern out of his voice. Why he felt worried, Clyde wasn't sure, but something didn't seem right.

He towered over Faith, and now worried she felt threatened by him. At least by his height. Clyde didn't believe his size was concerning to anyone, but one never knew. "Shall we sit and talk?" Leading her to the front pew, he ushered her in, and Faith complied. Clyde sat nearby.

She was pale and appeared more fragile than he recalled. Some people didn't cope well with the aftermath of the sessions he provided, but he didn't feel Faith was one of those. Or was it their earlier conversation that was upsetting her? "I told Molly," she blurted out, and her words surprised Clyde. Previously, she had decided not to tell her cousin.

"It's fine," he told her quietly. "It's your choice."

Faith stared at him, then blinked. "Not about the counseling," she said. "I told her..." She suddenly stopped talking and took a deep breath, letting it out so slowly Clyde thought she might faint. "I told her I was in love with you."

Clyde wasn't sure what he felt about her words. He stared into her face for a long moment, then suddenly stood. He glanced about, ensuring no one else was in earshot, but they were completely alone. "I..." How did he tell Faith he felt the same way? That until earlier today, he thought it was all one-sided? "I had planned to see the archbishop tomorrow," he whispered. "Or perhaps next week."

Confusion marred her face. "The archbishop? I…I don't understand."

Clyde sat down next to her again, then reached for her hands. "As you've probably realized by now, I have feelings for you, Faith. I'm uncertain what that means. I'm a preacher—it's my life calling."

Tears filled her eyes, but Faith blinked them back, then turned away. "I'm leaving town tomorrow," she said firmly. "I believe we were meant to be, but I guess circumstances don't allow it."

Clyde leaned in to ensure she could hear him. "God has a plan for us all," he whispered. "I firmly believe we were meant to be together." Clyde's heart pounded when he heard Faith gasp as she spun to face him. Was she upset at his declaration? She'd already declared her love for him, which confused him greatly.

"I shouldn't have come here," she said breathlessly. "It was a mistake. A huge mistake." She ran from the church, and Clyde stood, wishing he'd not told her his plans.

He didn't know how long he'd stood there, watching the door, hoping Faith would return. Eventually, he gave up and went to the parsonage. He should have done so to begin with. If he had, they wouldn't have had their discussion, and she wouldn't have decided to leave.

His shoulders slumped, and his heart hollow, Clyde went to the parsonage kitchen and made himself a cup of coffee. After that, he would have to buy supplies for supper. It was not something he looked forward to—an interrogation from Dennis, the unwelcomed matchmaker.

Chapter

Twelve

Faith stood outside the church, hot tears rolling down her face. She shouldn't have come back here. She'd gotten half way home, then felt compelled to return.

She could have slipped away quietly in the morning and not told Clyde. That way, he'd find out after she'd gone and it was too late to stop her.

Instead, she'd broken both their hearts.

If only Lucius hadn't been such an idiot. She should have known what he was like. Kissing her without permission all those years ago should have been a sign he was not to be trusted. Clyde had already told her it wasn't her fault. There are evil people in this world, and Lucius was one of them.

Swiping at her eyes, Faith began to walk away again. She wanted to run, but Dennis would see her and it would be all over town. It was the last thing she needed.

The church door opened, and she heard footsteps behind her. "Faith," Clyde said softly, surprise in his voice. "We need to talk. Please don't leave." He was upset—his expression made that perfectly clear. It was her fault. She'd upset him with her earlier declaration of love, and then telling him a short time later she was leaving town.

He had no choice but to come to the conclusion she was leaving because of him. Faith turned to face him. If they weren't outside and exposed to the town, and especially the prying eyes of Dennis, Faith may have run her fingers over his cheeks and through his neatly trimmed beard. Simply touching him was a comfort to her. Instead, she returned to the church as he had requested.

Clyde waved her into one of the pews at the back of the church. She could get outside quickly if needed, but she hoped it wouldn't come to that. "Promise me you won't leave town without talking to me first."

She could hear the emotion in his voice, and it cut at her heart. She didn't want to hurt this wonderful man, a man Faith knew she could love for the rest of her life. Instead of answering, she stared at him, her eyes filling with tears again. Not trusting herself to break down, instead of answering, she nodded.

Clyde sighed, then reached for her hand. "Come with me to see the archbishop. I will seek his blessing."

Her face felt stiff, and Faith knew she was torn. "Do you love me?" she asked in a whisper. Not once had he told her he loved her.

His eyes opened wide in astonishment. "I...of course I do. Didn't I say so just a short time ago?"

"No, you didn't," she said, tears now flooding her face. "You said we were meant to be together." Faith's heart was shattering. Did that mean the same thing as love? Possibly, but she wanted to be certain.

Clyde stared at her momentarily, then pulled her close. "Faith, I love you with all my heart. I have never said that to any woman before. Not ever."

His arms tightened around her, and Faith knew they were truly meant to be together. "I will accompany you to see the archbishop. Let me know when you plan to go," she whispered against his chest.

Clyde pushed her away and studied Faith for what seemed a lifetime. "Is tomorrow too soon?" She shook her head, and he continued. "I'll collect you after breakfast. It will be a long day for both of us."

Faith leaned into him again. She wanted to stay like this forever.

Faith was certain Molly knew something was wrong the moment she stepped inside. She pulled her cousin into the sitting room and sat her down. "What's going on?" she asked quietly. "You seem upset."

"Clyde loves me," Faith blurted out. She hadn't meant to say it in such a way, but what was done was done. "We're going to see the archbishop tomorrow." She twisted her hands in her lap, uncertain how Molly would take the news.

A sly smile crossed her lips. "Good," she said, then stood. "What time are you leaving?"

Faith stared at her cousin. Had she planned this all along? Clyde was a family friend, Faith knew that, but had there been plans afoot from the very beginning? "I don't understand," Faith said. "Have you been matchmaking?"

Her heart pounded. Was Marcus a part of this plan, too? Faith shook herself mentally. She had believed Dennis Andrews was the only matchmaker in town. It turned out her cousin had her own devious plans in place, too. This changed things—perhaps she should tell Clyde she was no longer going with him.

She stared up at Molly, who now frowned. "Why would you do such a thing? I trusted you, Molly."

Her cousin sat down again and reached for Faith's hand. "I did nothing. You and Clyde hit it off from the moment you met. I saw the chemistry between you in the church that first day."

Molly was right. Faith had felt it then, too. Apparently, so did Clyde, since he'd invited her to the diner. "We're leaving early in the morning. Straight after breakfast," Faith told her cousin.

It was then Molly stood. "Wash your face. We're going to invite Clyde for supper."

Faith didn't move. Was that such a good idea? Faith shook her head. "I'd rather not go with you," she whispered.

Molly frowned, but seemed to understand. "That's alright. Joey and I need fresh air." She smiled then, and Faith knew everything was going to turn out fine.

 Chapter

 Thirteen

Clyde stood outside the doctor's residence. Never had he felt so nervous to be coming here. Even supper with the family last night was difficult. For him, anyway. There was no doubt Marcus and Molly understood his intentions.

Now and then Marcus would grin, so Clyde assumed he was happy about the plans he and Faith had made. Would that make him part of this family? He'd always felt like family anyway, but marrying Faith would make it official.

He'd already collected his buggy from the livery and had a blanket ready for Faith. It would be a long day, and the cold will have set in before they returned home. Beyond that, they would stop to eat, both going to visit the archbishop, and returning.

He'd sent a telegraph to let the man know he would visit, so hopefully the long trip would not be in vain.

Finally, he knocked on the door. Clyde's heart pounded. Today could be life-changing. For both himself and for Faith.

Molly opened the door, then ushered him inside. "Faith won't be long. She's freshening up before the long trip." She indicated he should go into the sitting room and waited with him. "I packed some food for you," she said. "To keep you going until you can have a decent meal."

Clyde knew he shouldn't be surprised. This was Molly—she loved to cook, and loved her family even more. "Thank you. We appreciate it," he told her.

Molly grinned, and it took a moment for him to realize what had caused it. He went over his words in his mind. No longer did he talk in the singular, it was the plural—*we*. Was it wrong he thought of himself and Faith as a couple now? Clyde didn't think so. He was certain Molly didn't either.

Clyde heard footsteps coming down the hallway, and his heart fluttered. When the sound stopped, his heart sank. Marcus stood in the doorway and grinned. "Good luck today," he said. Before Clyde could answer, he was gone.

Soon he heard not only dainty footsteps, but the quivering of a gown being lifted. This time, he was certain Faith was on her way. When she entered the sitting room she was huffing, she was so breathless. "You shouldn't have rushed," Clyde said, standing to go to her.

Instead of answering, she gave him a wry smile. "Too late," she said breathlessly, then sat to regain her composure. They sat quietly until her breathing had calmed down.

Molly had left the room moments earlier and now returned with a large paper bag. "Some snacks," she said, handing it over to Clyde. "Should we expect you for supper?"

Shaking his head, Clyde answered. "I doubt it. If we're back that early, we'll eat at the diner."

"I can save something for you," Molly insisted.

"Please don't. It is far too much trouble. Besides, I do not know what time we'll arrive back." It was then it hit him. "I wonder if we should take an overnight bag?" He was thinking out loud and hadn't meant to speak the words.

He glanced across at Molly and saw a look of horror on her face. Faith wasn't much different. If it hadn't been so serious, it would have been laughable.

"You're not getting married today," Molly said firmly. "I want to be at my cousin's wedding."

That hadn't been the plan at all. "I…I don't believe so. I only suggested an overnight bag in case we are caught up and have to stay the night."

Molly and Faith glanced at each other before facing Clyde again. "Separate rooms, I hope!" Molly said, a modicum of shock in her voice.

"Of course," Clyde said, trying to keep the annoyance from his voice. "I'll wait outside for you, Faith, while you pack a bag." He stood and left the house. The fresh air would do him good.

Clyde didn't have to wait long, but was already annoyed with himself by the time Faith came out. Her displeasure was clear, and he wondered if she still planned to accompany him. "I apologize," he told Faith as she closed the front door. "I am normally far more patient than that. I'm eager to see the archbishop, I suppose."

Faith's face softened. "As I am," she said, then smiled. She handed him a small overnight bag, which he stowed under the seat of the buggy. "Did you pack a bag?"

He pointed next to her bag. "I always have a packed bag stowed away. I never know what circumstances might present themselves. Are you ready?"

When Faith nodded, he held her around the waist and assisted her into the buggy, then climbed up next to her. The folded blanket between them felt like a barrier, which only added to his concerns.

Clyde hoped their trip today would wipe away any fears he was harnessing. He wasn't sure what he would do if it didn't.

As they pulled into the driveway, Clyde breathed a sigh of relief. Neither of them had spoken much along the way, except here and there. He didn't want to pre-empt their meeting with Archbishop Angus Tully, for fear it may upset Faith.

He had no clue how his news would be taken. Without the blessing of the archbishop, they couldn't marry. And that would be a travesty.

The front door of the large house opened as he came to a stop and pulled on the brake. Clyde helped Faith down and introduced her. Archbishop Tully seemed cordial enough, although he didn't know why they'd come to see him. Clyde didn't mention that in his correspondence, only the fact he needed to speak with the man.

"It's good to see you again, Clyde," he said, offering his hand. "And who might this young lady be?" He winked at Clyde as though he had already guessed the reason for their visit.

"Archbishop Tully, this is Faith Cavendish. We would like to get married." Clyde noted it did not surprise the archbishop at his declaration.

"Angus, please." He turned to Faith then. "Very nice to meet you, Faith. It is alright if I call you Faith?"

"Of course," she said with a smile, then offered her hand for him to shake.

He lifted his hand, and an older man emerged. "Buck will take care of your horse. You two come inside and freshen up."

When Clyde returned to the sitting room where they were instructed to wait, Faith was already there and talking with Angus. They appeared to be getting along fine. It was an immense relief to Clyde.

"Ah, Clyde," Angus said. "Your young lady and I have been getting to know each other." He turned and smiled at Faith. "You have done well for yourself," he said, his tone still friendly. Clyde felt it had to be a good sign. "What plans have you made for your future?" Now he was getting down to the matter at hand.

"We've made no plans at this stage," Clyde told him. "I wanted to speak with you first." He reached across and took Faith's hand. Although she might appear relaxed, he knew better and could see she was terrified.

It was then a maid entered the room carrying a pot of tea and three cups. "Thank you, Mildred," Angus said. "I'll play mother." He smiled at the woman, who then left the room. "Unless you'd rather do it, Faith?" He smiled again, and Clyde felt certain this was a test for Faith.

Sliding forward in her chair, it seemed Faith was a wake up to him. "Of course. I'd be honored." She began pouring the tea, leaving enough room for milk and sugar. She handed the first cup to Angus, who winked at Clyde.

He knew it! Clyde knew it was a test. "You'll do a lot of this sort of thing as a preacher's wife," Angus said gently. "The preacher's wife is very important not only to the preacher, but to the entire community."

Faith nodded, then offered Angus a cookie. It took all Clyde's effort to resist sighing. Today was going to be trying, not only for him, but mostly for Faith. He should have known. If he had, Clyde would have warned Faith. Although she seemed to handle it very well.

Chapter

Fourteen

Clyde was banished while Angus talked to Faith about being a preacher's wife. He explained the responsibilities she would need to undertake. Things like helping the Ladies' Auxiliary, hosting lunches, morning and afternoon teas. There would also be times she would need to step in and talk to distraught women when they didn't want to speak with a man.

That part she could totally relate to.

As Angus outlined the various tasks, Faith felt overwhelmed. Then suddenly she didn't. "I can handle anything that's thrown my way," she said, believing every word.

The archbishop sat back in his chair. "I believe you can." He slapped his hands against his knees. "You look tired, my dear." He reached across and rang a bell. "Mildred," he said as the maid entered the room. "Run a bath for Miss Cavendish would you? I'm sure she would love to wash away all the grit and dust from her travels." He turned to Faith then. "You brought an overnight bag, didn't you?" His eyebrows rose as he waited for an answer.

"I did. Clyde insisted." But why did she need an overnight bag?

"Excellent," he answered as he rubbed his hands together. He then glanced toward the entrance of the sitting room. "Ah, you're back, Clyde. Perfect timing." He motioned Clyde to sit down. Clyde already appeared far more relaxed. His walk must have done some good. "I've arranged a bath for Faith. You will stay tonight, won't you? Your rooms are ready and waiting for you."

Confusion filled Faith. Everything seemed to go well. Why did they need to stay overnight? Had she assessed the situation incorrectly? Her heart sank.

"Thank you, Angus. That sounds wonderful." Clyde stepped toward Faith and put an arm around her, then kissed her cheek. "A bath sounds good," he said, then sat nearby.

He discreetly nodded at her, and Faith almost missed it. Was he trying to tell her everything was going well? Or was he simply trying to encourage her to leave the men alone? Faith was more confused than ever, but she took the hint when Mildred returned.

"Follow me, Miss," the maid said. "You have a splendid bathroom," she said, then smiled at Faith. Did the maid mean the archbishop had a magnificent bathroom? The woman's words confused her. Faith followed along without comment. "Here we are, Miss. This is the best of the guest rooms." She closed the door behind them. "Your bath is through that door. Leave your clothes here on this chair, and I will launder them. Where is your overnight bag?"

"Oh!" Faith said. She'd totally forgotten about it. "I believe it's in the buggy. I'll collect it." She spun around to go back downstairs. "You don't need to launder my clothes. They'll be fine."

"I will collect your bag while you bathe. Let me help you." The young maid began to help Faith out of her clothes. She'd never had such an encounter before. Many women may have enjoyed the experience, but Faith decided it was not for her, and stopped the maid from removing her undergarments. Mildred did not argue with the decision. "Take your time," Mildred said. "There's no hurry."

Mildred left her alone, and Faith breathed a sigh of relief. She finished undressing, then slid into the bath filled with hot water and lots of fragrant bubbles. Faith decided Mildred was worth her weight in gold.

Faith glanced around the bathroom Mildred had described as splendid. There was no disputing it— she had never witnessed such beauty before. She lay back in the equally splendid bathtub and contemplated her situation. It was becoming increasingly clear if Angus didn't approve of her, he would not allow the marriage to take place. Where would that leave them?

When she was finished bathing, she would try to get Clyde alone. Did he have an alternative plan if Angus denied their request? She wondered if he could even do such a thing. Faith had no idea of the etiquette in such a situation.

The water was now tepid, so Faith decided it was time to finish. There was a tap at the door, and then it opened just a crack. "May I enter, Miss?" Mildred's voice was gentle, as though she understood Faith's modesty. "I have a towel for you."

"You may," Faith said, still unsure. Mildred then entered and opened up a huge, white, fluffy towel. She stood there, facing away, as Faith stood and stepped into the towel, which the maid then wrapped around her.

She had never used such a luxurious towel in her life. Faith was beginning to understand the draw some people had to wealth, but she vowed to never to fall into that trap. "Thank you, Mildred," she said, and the other woman smiled, then left her alone.

After drying herself, Faith went back to the luxurious bedroom. The clothes from her overnight bag were laid out on the bed, ready for her to dress. Her soiled clothes were gone, despite her insisting Mildred need not worry. Still, she couldn't complain—the maid was merely doing her job.

Faith dried her blonde hair as much as possible, then fashioned it into what she believed would be an acceptable style. She then prepared to go back downstairs.

As she stepped out onto the top stair, Faith heard muffled voices coming from the sitting room. It was enough to make her pause. By suggesting she would enjoy a bath to wash away the grit of the trip, was Angus trying to get her out of the way for a while? She wondered if he was now suggesting Clyde shouldn't marry her. Faith knew her mind was in a spin, but everything had happened so quickly.

One minute she was being counseled by Clyde, and the next they were making plans to marry. They hadn't even known each other very long.

The thought made her pause. Should they even be contemplating marriage this early in their relationship? It seemed like forever ago, but it was only yesterday they'd declared their love for each other.

Faith's heart sank. If Angus discovered that piece of information, would he send them away to think about it longer? Tears filled her eyes, but Faith was determined not to let them fall. They were both adults, and more than capable of making this decision for themselves. If Clyde hadn't been a preacher, they would have decided without intervention.

Suddenly, she was determined. She straightened her shoulders and stormed down the stairs as she fought back her tears. Instead of tears of sadness, they had turned into tears of anger. The Grandfather clock in the entrance chimed as she reached the bottom.

Mildred stood there, looking up at her. The young maid smiled. "You look lovely, Miss," she said sweetly. And with those few words, her anger disappeared.

"Thank you, Mildred," she said, then headed into the sitting room, prepared for anything.

#

#

Both men stood as Faith entered the room. She straightened her shoulders, although the walk down the stairs had lessened her inner turmoil.

Angus stepped toward her. "You look beautiful, Faith. If you weren't already taken…" he let the words trail off, and although Clyde knew he was joking, he felt a twinge of jealousy.

"She certainly does," Clyde said, reaching for her hand. "Do you feel better after your bath?" Faith looked radiant and had Angus not been in the room, he would have told her so. There was nothing like having a witness to your conversations to put a damper on things.

Mildred stepped into the room. "Supper will be served in fifteen minutes," she announced, then left the room as quietly as she'd entered it.

Angus rubbed his hands together. "That gives us a little time to complete our discussions. Please, Faith," he said, indicating a chair. "Do sit down."

Faith sat, then glanced across at Clyde.

"I have made my decision," Angus announced, clapping his hands together.

Clyde's nerves were at breaking point.

"I can see how much you two are in love. I give my approval for the marriage to go ahead. In fact," he continued, now standing next to the mantle, "I can perform the ceremony tomorrow before you return home."

"Oh!" Faith's exclamation had both men pivoting toward her.

Angus frowned. "You don't want me to marry you tomorrow, Faith?" He seemed disappointed, and so was Clyde, but he understood Faith's reluctance.

"We have friends and family who would want to attend the ceremony," Clyde said firmly. "Faith's cousin, for one. She has allowed Faith to stay with her since she moved to Crystal Springs."

Angus glanced from one to the other of them. "I see," he said, and Clyde could almost see his mind ticking over. "Perhaps I should come to Crystal Springs and perform the ceremony. How does a week from Saturday sound?"

"It sounds perfect," Clyde answered. He glanced across at Faith to find her beaming.

It seemed like only moments later when Mildred returned to escort them to supper. Clyde had visited here before, but he reveled in watching Faith's reaction to the stunning dining room. At first glance, the entire building seemed overkill, but Angus often hosted meetings and Bible studies here, not to mention visiting dignitaries. His home was more like a mansion, but Clyde knew he could not live in such a place. His home was humble and suitable for his needs. He hoped and prayed Faith was of the same mind, especially after being pampered here by Angus's staff, especially Mildred.

He held Faith's hand as her eyes scanned the room. The high ceilings with their carved artistry were exquisite. The table was set as though for a king. Clyde had seen it all before, but it still took his breath away.

Faith gasped as she took it all in. "This room, it's magnificent," she managed to say, her voice full of emotion.

Angus smiled. "It is a true work of art," he replied, then indicated for them to take their seats. Once they were all seated, he turned to Faith. "This building belonged to Thomas Grayden. He was the richest man of his time. His wealth didn't bring happiness, only gold diggers. As a result, he never married. Thomas Grayden left his home to the church, along with all his money and worldly possessions."

Faith's eyes opened wide in astonishment. "That's really sad," she said. "Everyone deserves love." She turned to Clyde and smiled tentatively. He could see Angus's story had upset her, but she also reveled in her surroundings.

"Pumpkin soup," Mildred announced as she placed a large ceramic terrine on the table, then served it into individual bowls. She placed the first bowl in front of Faith, then Clyde, and last, Angus was served.

"Let us pray," Angus said, and bowed his head. The others followed suit. "Lord, thank you for this food and all you have set before us. I pray you will watch over Clyde and Faith, and allow their love to continue to grow. May they have a long and happy life together. Amen."

When Faith lifted her head, Clyde saw tears swimming in her eyes. The words Angus said were moving and had apparently affected Faith far more than he expected.

"Shall we begin?" Angus asked and indicated for Faith to start.

She took a tentative mouthful. "Oh, it's delicious," she said, surprise filling her voice.

Angus gave her a nod in acknowledgement, and the men then began to eat. Clyde had learned a lot about Faith today—she was far more worldly than he'd expected. She fitted in to both worlds, the one at Crystal Springs, and here amongst wealth as was necessary. His soon-to-be wife was a chameleon, and he didn't mind one bit.

After supper, they moved into the parlor. The men drank coffee, while Faith preferred tea. Clyde was so full he felt he wouldn't need to eat for another week. Angus was the perfect host, but Clyde knew that already.

"If you don't mind," Faith said when she finished her tea, "I will retire for the night. It's been a long day."

Angus stood and helped Faith to her feet. "I'm sure it has," he said. "The long trip here would have been enough to wear anyone out."

Clyde also stood. "I'll accompany you to your room." He turned to Angus then. "You don't mind, do you? I'll return in a few minutes."

"Of course," Angus told him. "I'll be waiting."

Clyde hooked Faith's arm through his and they left the room, then ascended the stairs. "This is my room," Faith said. She leaned in and whispered. "It's the most decadent room I've ever seen, let alone stayed in. It even has its own bathroom, with running water and a bath!" she declared.

Clyde couldn't help but laugh. He'd never had the good fortune to sleep in that particular room, but he had seen it. He was given the grand tour the last time he visited here, which was some time ago. "Don't get used to it," he said, trying to keep the laughter out of his voice.

Faith stared up at him. "It's nice to visit, but I wouldn't want to live here." She tried to stifle a yawn, but failed miserably.

"I will leave you to sleep. Goodnight, my darling," Clyde said as he pulled her close and wrapped his arms around her. When she glanced up and studied him, Clyde kissed her gently. He couldn't wait to marry her, his soulmate.

In a little over a week, they would be man and wife. What the rest of their lives held, only God knew. "I love you," he whispered as she walked into the room. He wasn't sure Faith heard him.

 Chapter

 Sixteen

Faith awoke to her curtains being opened. Mildred was no doubt following orders, and at least she didn't fling them back hurriedly. It was a gentle awakening, which Faith appreciated.

"Good morning, Miss," Mildred said, then helped Faith to sit up, placing an additional pillow behind her head. "Are you going down to breakfast? You can choose to have breakfast in bed if you'd rather."

"Breakfast in bed? That's so decadent!" She was shocked at the thought, and declined the offer. "What time is it, please, Mildred?" Faith stretched her arms and yawned. She felt half asleep. Hopefully that would change after she washed her face in cold water.

"It's almost seven, Miss," Mildred told her. "Preacher Walters said you had a long trip and would leave after breakfast this morning." Mildred seemed sad at the knowledge they were leaving. "I've enjoyed having you here, Miss. I do hope you visit again."

As Faith climbed out of the bed, Mildred helped her into a robe. "I've laundered your clothes, Miss. I thought you might wish to wear them this morning." Mildred smiled at her, and Faith felt compelled to pull the young girl into a hug. What an awful life she must have—a life of servitude, and little to show for it.

"Do you live here, Mildred?" Faith asked. She had no idea why she asked—the words seemed to have a life of their own.

"Oh yes, Miss. The servants' quarters are in the basement. It's not like the old days, though. We are well looked after here. There aren't many of us anymore. The need isn't there."

"Do you have a boyfriend, Mildred?" Faith asked.

Heat crept into the young woman's face. "I do, but Archbishop Tully cannot know," she whispered, as though the walls had ears. "He works here too. We plan to marry next year, but we haven't told anyone." Suddenly she appeared worried. "I don't know if we'll be allowed to stay on."

"Your secret is safe with me," Faith assured her. "Thank you for trusting me."

Mildred smiled and left her to freshen up and dress. As much as she loved this place, she'd much rather be back in Crystal Springs where she could relax and not have to comply with rules or have servants helping with her every move.

Soon Faith found herself descending the stairs. She followed the men's voices to the dining room. They both stood as she entered.

"Good morning, Faith," Angus said. "Help yourself to whatever takes your fancy."

"Thank you," she said, then stepped toward Clyde. He placed a light kiss on her forehead.

"I trust you slept well?" he asked, his arms encircling her momentarily. "You appear well rested."

It almost felt like she was living a dream. "The bed was incredibly comfortable. And Mildred," she turned to Angus then. "She is an absolute gem."

"She is," Angus said. "Don't you go stealing her from me." He laughed at his own joke, then finally sat back down.

"It has been lovely to visit here, Angus. Never before have I experienced such luxury," Faith said as she helped herself to pancakes and strawberries from the sideboard. Never had she eaten such a decadent breakfast. And more than likely, she never would again. "I can honestly say it's not something I would relish."

Angus laughed again. "It is something you become accustomed to," he told her, then lifted his cup of coffee and sipped it.

She glanced at Clyde. He was smiling, but said not a word.

The moment Faith joined them at the table, a cup of tea was placed in front of her. It seemed the treatment she'd received since the moment they arrived would continue until they left.

"I plan to leave after breakfast," Clyde said. "We have a long trip ahead of us." His empty plate was swept away as he spoke.

"I wish you could stay longer," Angus said. "I have enjoyed Faith's company." He turned to Clyde then, a grin on his face. "And yours too, of course."

"Why wouldn't you?" Clyde said. "Sadly, for you, she is already spoken for." Clyde reached across the table and covered Faith's hand. He smiled at her then, and warmth filled her.

"I am an old man," Angus said, waving a hand in front of himself. "One wife is enough for me."

"You're married?" Faith said, shock filling her.

"Widowed, I'm afraid. My dear wife, Rebecca, died from fever only a few years after we married."

Faith was crying inside. "My deepest condolences," she said, and meant every word.

"It was a very long time ago. Let's not dwell on it, but plan for your upcoming nuptials instead."

It was the best idea Faith had heard all day.

After hugging her tightly and shaking Clyde's hands, Angus stood watching as they drove back toward home. Sadness covered his face, and Faith felt as though she was farewelling a good friend. Reminding herself he would travel to Crystal Springs in a little over a week to marry them was the only thing that consoled her.

It was the strangest thing. She had known the archbishop for less than a day, and yet she had a feeling of deep loss.

"He gets under your skin, doesn't he?" Clyde said. It was as though he could read her thoughts. "It's what makes him so good at his job."

Faith contemplated him. "I felt enamored with Angus almost the moment we met. I wonder if he knows how he makes people feel?"

Clyde chuckled. "He knows and uses it frequently." His statement confused Faith. "Angus is particularly good at fundraising. He can easily convince a benefactor to part with their money for the sake of the church." He turned to study her, and she shivered.

It felt as though he was trying to look inside her head. And yet, Clyde knew all there was to know about her. She had told him her innermost secrets. Some parts, even Molly didn't know.

"Thank you for bringing me here," Faith said. "And for helping me with…" she shrugged her shoulders. "You know." She glanced down into her lap then, her hands clasped tightly together.

Clyde reached over and covered her hands. "Are you alright? I know it's been a stressful couple of days."

"More for you than me, I imagine," she told him. "Mildred ensured I was pampered. For a while there, it felt like I was one of those rich ladies living the high life." Faith laughed, and Clyde joined her. "It's really not my style. I will be thrilled to be back in Crystal Springs, living an ordinary life, with my ordinary friends and family."

"I hope you've included me in that list," Clyde said, then winked.

"Without you, there is no point in staying," Faith said, and meant every word.

Chapter

Seventeen

Dennis stood sweeping the boardwalk outside the mercantile when they arrived back in town. He stopped and watched them drive past. Clyde could barely withhold a snicker, but in his position, it was not something he should do.

Faith, on the other hand, waved to the town matchmaker, and smiled. "You are so wicked," Clyde told her. "But I do love you."

They continued on until they reached the Ryan house. As if she was nervously awaiting their arrival, Molly opened the front door, little Joey in her arms. "Welcome back," she said. Moments later, Clyde had helped Faith to the ground, and she was fully embraced by Molly and her son. "Well?" Molly asked impatiently.

"The archbishop offered to marry us there and then."

Molly's face dropped.

"Except he didn't," Clyde quickly added. He was glad they insisted on marrying here in town.

Molly let out a long sigh of relief. "Thank goodness," she said, then turned to Faith again. "You had me worried for a minute there."

"Angus is coming to town and will marry us on Saturday," Faith told her cousin.

"Saturday? That's not enough time," Molly said, panic rising in her voice.

"Next Saturday," Clyde informed her. "Perhaps you two ladies should sit and talk. I'll take the buggy back to the livery, then return." He studied Molly then. "If you wish for me to return, that is."

"Yes, of course. We have much to discuss. Come on, Faith. I'm sure you're ready for a break." The two women headed inside, and Clyde headed toward the livery. Although the buggy and his horse Roger belonged to the church, they were stored at the livery when not in use. It meant Roger was well fed, properly cared for, and was given the exercise he needed. It gave Clyde peace of mind.

After settling Roger into his stall, Clyde strolled back to see Molly and Faith. They were no doubt planning for the upcoming nuptials. It got Clyde to thinking about the parsonage. Was it suitable for a wife? Did he need to make adjustments?

Perhaps he needed to get Molly's opinion. It would need to be sooner than later.

Suddenly, he stopped walking. Did he even have time to arrange for Molly to check for him? Suddenly, he was startled by shouting.

"Hey, Clyde!" Dennis called to him from the boardwalk he'd been sweeping earlier. "Is everything alright?"

Clyde squinted. What was Dennis doing sweeping this far along the boardwalk? He rarely swept anyway, letting his teenage workers do it instead. Now he was as far down as the butcher's shop. "Hello, Dennis," he called back. Although frustrating, Dennis did no one any harm. At least not intentionally. "I'm just going for a stroll."

Suddenly Dennis was by his side, broom still in his hands. "I noticed you driving into town a while ago," he said, no doubt trying to find out what was going on.

"That's right," Clyde said. "Now, if you'll excuse me, Dennis, I have errands to run." He began to walk away.

"Did Faith enjoy the trip?" Dennis then asked, still trying to extract vital information. Vital to Dennis anyway.

"She did, thank you. Now I really must go," Clyde said and walked faster than he remembered having done before. It wasn't that they were keeping it secret, but he and Faith would make an announcement when it suited them. Not when Dennis was ready to spread his gossip.

He shouldn't be angry with Dennis. The man was lonely, and Clyde knew full well what that was like. Not for the first time, he felt Dennis needed someone to keep him company. Perhaps it was time the townsfolk got together and worked something out.

Finally, back at Molly's, Clyde knocked on the door. "Come in," Molly called from the sitting room. He figured they'd seen him cross the road and past the window. "How did you get away from Dennis?" Molly laughed and although annoyed at the matchmaker, Clyde could see the funny side.

He shook his head at the memory. "The man is a pest. Can you please match him up with someone, Molly? Get him off all our backs?" He wasn't really serious, but Clyde knew it was the perfect solution. "If we don't get an announcement out about our nuptials soon, Dennis is sure to make something up."

He sat on the sofa next to Faith, where he held her hand. Faith leaned into him. "It's little more than a week. Surely he can't get into too much mischief in that short a time?"

Clyde rolled his eyes. "I wouldn't bet on it," he said, then sat back, trying to calm himself down. He wanted the wedding to go to plan without interference, and he wasn't sure that could be accomplished with Dennis hovering the way he did.

Marcus sat in the church office as they waited for Molly's assessment. Faith cleaned the church while they all waited. She'd insisted on going with Molly, but her cousin was having none of it.

"I'm nervous," Clyde whispered, worried Faith might hear. "I've never so much as dated a woman until Faith came along."

"In that case," Marcus told him, "you're doing particularly well." He grinned at his friend, and Clyde knew Marcus was stirring him up. "You'll do fine. Let me know if you need any instructions on having a happy marriage."

Clyde frowned. "Isn't that my job—counseling newlyweds or about to be married couples?"

"It is," Marcus said, unable to halt his laughter. "Have you found a way to counsel yourself?"

It had been obvious almost from the moment they'd announced their marriage plans that Marcus was going to stir him up, but Clyde didn't think it would be quite this bad.

Suddenly the door opened, and Molly entered, a sheet of paper in her hand. Clyde mentally slapped himself. "Tell me the damage," he mumbled. They still had a few days to fix all the issues.

She handed Clyde the list. "It's really only the kitchen. You need far more cooking utensils, and food. Your pantry is near empty! Oh, and some feminine soaps for the bathroom would be nice." Exasperation was clear in her voice. "Do you trust me to sort it out for you? Faith might like a hand in stocking both kitchen and pantry as well."

It was a dilemma he wasn't sure how to answer. Instead of dealing with it, Clyde sat rigid, hoping the problem would go away.

"Right," Molly said, then stepped to the doorway of the church. "Faith, do you have a moment?" Without another word, the women left Clyde's office and headed toward the mercantile.

"Now you've done it," Marcus told him. "Giving Molly free rein is never a good idea."

Confusion clouded Clyde's mind. "I…did I do that? I don't recall…"

"Don't worry about it," Marcus assured him. "Molly has it all in hand."

The gravity of that finally hit, and Clyde groaned.

The moment Faith and Molly stepped inside the mercantile, both women regretted it. Dennis was at the counter in record time. No doubt he'd seen the comings and goings at the church and wanted to know what was going on.

"Good morning, ladies," he said cordially. A sure sign he was on alert. "What can I do for you today?"

Faith studied him momentarily, then relaxed somewhat. "I'm after some kitchen utensils," she said, trying to keep her voice sturdy. "I also need food and bathroom supplies."

It was Dennis's turn to study her. "You'll need a box then?" he asked, curiosity written all over his face. "I thought you were only here for a holiday." Now suspicion covered his face. And suddenly reality hit him. "You're getting married! It must be…" He was thoughtful for a minute, not saying a word. Then the answer apparently came to him. "It's the preacher! I knew it. I predicted it from the start, and I was right." The man now wore a smug grin.

Trying to keep her composure intact, Faith turned to her cousin. "Come on, Molly. Let's see what's up the back of the store. Or maybe we should get the buggy and drive to…" She didn't have the chance to finish the sentence before Dennis was all apologies.

"No, no," he said hurriedly. "I have plenty of kitchen supplies here. Better than anywhere else in a fifty-mile radius." He wore a smile now, instead of appearing smug. Faith found him so frustrating, as did many of the townsfolk. Apart from his matchmaking antics, Dennis Andrews was a good person. So it was easy to forgive him—until the next escapade.

Dennis snatched up a large box. "Would you like me to come with you, or would you prefer to shop alone?"

"Whatever you prefer," Faith said with a shrug. She immediately knew that was the wrong answer. She glanced across at the list of items Clyde had in his kitchen already and picked some of the missing utensils off the shelf. Then she turned to Molly. "He really doesn't have a wooden spoon? Nor a sieve?" Faith closed her eyes, then placed both items in the cardboard box Dennis carried beside them. She purchased several other utensils, like an oven tray for biscuits, a cake tin, and a rolling pin. When Faith was happy with the kitchen supplies, they moved into the bathroom stores.

Molly picked up two cakes of lavender soap for her cousin to use, then reached for a container of bath salts. "Oh, I couldn't," Faith said, putting the bath salts back on the shelf.

"He has an enormous bath, with running water," Molly whispered, knowing full well Faith loved a good bath.

Faith groaned.

"I'll give you a discount for the bath salts," Dennis said. "It will be my wedding gift."

Faith resisted the urge to roll her eyes. She was probably saving ten cents. Twenty at the most. Besides, she hadn't confirmed they were getting married, although it was probably all around town by now. But if Dennis didn't know, perhaps no one else did. They would soon, knowing Dennis.

The thought irked her, but, as Molly said, she enjoyed a good long soak. "I had a lovely bath at the archbishop's place," Faith said, remembering how luxurious it was.

Dennis quirked an eyebrow. "Archbishop Tully?" A sly grin alerted Faith to the fact she'd inadvertently confirmed their marriage.

Molly elbowed her, but it was too late. Dennis knew, and now the whole town would know. They might as well put a sign in the mercantile window.

The pair finished their shopping and left Dennis to write up the account and deliver their purchases to the parsonage. He promised to do that after the store closed.

Faith hoped Clyde didn't think she'd gone overboard.

The next few days passed in a whirlwind of organization. If there was one thing Molly was good at, that was coordinating whatever needed doing. It was one of the reasons she'd done so well at the bakery, according to Marcus.

Sitting at the kitchen table, Molly had lists. Several of them. One for food, one for Faith's outfit, and another for guests. Why she bothered with a guest list Faith didn't know. Once the word was out, and by now it would be, thanks to Dennis, everyone would flock to the church at the given time.

"I have asked Joel to make the pastries for the wedding," Molly told her. "He's agreed, but only if that can be his wedding gift to you both."

Faith clapped her hands with glee. "How wonderful," she said. "I'll make a note to thank him personally."

"Oh, and he's also gifting the wedding cake."

"I barely even know Joel," Faith said. "That is incredibly generous of him."

Molly smiled. "Everyone knows and loves Clyde. They'll all get to know you, too."

She knew Molly was right, but it was all quite overwhelming. Another few days and she would be a married woman. Who knew when she came to visit her cousin that Faith would meet her soulmate? She closed her eyes and said a silent prayer of thanks. Without His plan, she wouldn't be sitting here now.

Molly lay her pencil on the table and studied her cousin. Faith fidgeted under her gaze. "I didn't tell you sooner because I wanted it to be a surprise, but Alice Goldie is making your wedding dress," she said.

"Alice? Do I know her?" Faith asked. She was still getting to know everyone in town.

"You met her at church. Alice is the town dressmaker. Your wedding outfit is a gift from Marcus and I."

Faith shook her head vigorously. "You are already doing far too much," Faith objected.

"It's done. We've already paid her, so there's nothing you can do about it." Molly raised her eyebrows, daring Faith to argue. She knew better— Molly always won.

A moment later, there was a knock at the door. "That will be Alice," Molly said, then headed to the door. Faith knew it would be a long few days until the wedding.

Faith handed her bouquet to Molly as she arrived at the altar. Clyde stood staring at her. She hoped he liked what he saw. One thing she knew for certain, her gown was stunning. Alice had done an amazing job. Made with pale blue taffeta and matching lace, Faith felt like a queen walking down the aisle. She wore a small hat of the same material, and a small veil that covered only her eyes.

Clyde seemed spellbound. "You look stunning," he whispered as he leaned in. He then reached for her hand.

Archbishop Tully, Angus, stood before them, a wry smile on his face. Faith was delighted he would be the one to marry them. She was pleased she'd gotten to know him before today. Being married by a complete stranger would not be the same.

Angus cleared his throat. He opened the well-worn Bible in his hands and began the ceremony. "We are gathered here today to join this man and woman in holy matrimony. Before we begin, are there any objections?" Under his breath, Faith heard him say *there better not be any*. He glanced down at Faith and grinned. His words were meant only for Clyde and herself. Marcus and Molly quietly chuckled, so it was apparent they'd heard his grumblings as well.

The rest of the service went in a blur, and Faith could barely remember a word that was said. Except when it came to the part where each of them had to say *I do* as they clasped the other's hands.

Her heart fluttered, knowing she and Clyde were joined forever, never to be torn apart. As they walked down the aisle and outside the entrance of the church, Clyde kissed her before everyone streamed outside. It was a chaste kiss, but one she would remember forever.

Their first kiss as man and wife.

Epilogue

Ten months later…

Clyde sat quietly in the parsonage's parlor. He smiled across at Faith, who had come into her own as the preacher's wife.

She poured the last cup of tea for the women's Bible study group and offered oatmeal cookies to each of their guests.

"These are delicious, Faith," Molly told her.

Listening and watching had become Clyde's favorite past-time. He adored watching his wife as she settled into each new role that had been forced on her, and every new challenge she faced.

Faith had become an important part of Crystal Springs, bringing people together and introducing them to the word of God. She formed and sang in the church choir, and her angelic voice stirred his heart every time she sang.

How he'd lived without her, Clyde would never know.

"Let me get some pound cake," Faith said. "I meant to cut that beforehand."

Martha Evans studied Faith. "You've done enough, Faith. Next time I'll bring pastries from the bakery. Joel won't mind."

Clyde was certain she was right.

As she went to stand, Faith's face tensed. She bent forward, then screamed. Molly was on her feet in seconds, as was Clyde. "Go get Marcus," Molly demanded of him. "The baby is coming."

Confusion clouded his mind, but only for mere seconds. Molly put her hands to his shoulders. "Marcus is in his office. Get him now!" A gentle shove had Clyde heading toward his destination.

He near ran to the doctor's office. The door was closed when he arrived, and the waiting area had a few people seated. Clyde couldn't sit, and he couldn't stand still. Then he pounded on the door. "Marcus," he shouted through the door, but got no response. He waited a few minutes before repeating the action. "Marcus," he called even louder than before.

Finally, the door opened. "Clyde?" he said, surprised. "What's the emergency?" He reached out and steadied his friend, who was still on edge.

"The baby is coming," he said, his voice sounded unsteady, even to Clyde.

"I'm sorry, everyone. I have to see to this baby."
Marcus grabbed his medical bag and went with
Clyde, leaving his patients behind. The few people
there clapped. Pride ran through Clyde's veins.

"It will be alright," Marcus said. "Women give birth
all the time."

"Women die all the time giving birth," Clyde
grumbled, concerned for his wife.

Marcus stopped walking and faced his friend.
"Clyde," he said firmly. "Not on my watch." He
said, then continued to the parsonage. Clyde's fears
were allayed, for now at least.

"Congratulations, Clyde," Marcus said some hours
later. "It's a girl." He handed the baby over to
Clyde, and he quickly had a group of women
surrounding him.

"Give him some space," Molly demanded, then
moved in closer herself. "She is beautiful," Molly
said, running a finger softly down the baby's cheek.

"Is Faith...?" Words failed him. Clyde was grateful
his daughter had arrived unscathed, but he needed
assurance his wife was in good health, too.

"Faith is fine. She's in perfect condition. Do you
honestly think I'd let anything happen to her? Molly
would never let me hear the end of it. Besides, I

have never lost a mother or baby yet. I don't intend to ever let that happen."

"Thank you," Clyde whispered. "Can I see Faith now?"

"Of course," Marcus answered. "Be aware she is exhausted."

Molly took the baby out of Clyde's arms and stared down into her tiny face. She did what Clyde should have done, but his concern at that moment was with his wife. He'd spent most of her labor praying for Faith to pull through.

God had answered his prayers.

Clyde moved as quietly as he could into the bedroom. Faith lay sleeping, and he didn't want to disturb her, but needed to assure himself she was healthy, as Marcus had said. He carefully sat on the edge of the bed.

"Clyde," Faith whispered. "Where is the baby? Is she alright?" Panic showed on her face.

Clyde reached out and brushed back her hair. "Molly is holding her. Marcus said you needed to rest." He leaned in and kissed her forehead. "She is beautiful, like her mother." His heart was full of joy. If they never had another child, it would be fine with Clyde. The terror he felt all those hours Faith was birthing their daughter were pure hell.

Pulling up the covers to ensure Faith was warm enough, Clyde leaned over and kissed her again. Life with Faith was good. More than good, it was wonderful. He said a silent prayer of thanks to God for getting her through, and for the safe delivery of their daughter.

He also thanked God for carrying out His plans for Faith and himself. Clyde was more than content with his life as a married man. He was also more than thankful he could still spread the word of God.

From the Author

Thank you so much for reading my book – I hope you enjoyed it.

I would greatly appreciate you leaving a review where you purchased, even if it is only a one-liner. It helps to have my books more visible!

~*~

Multi-published, award-winning and bestselling author Cheryl Wright, former secretary, debt collector, account manager, writing coach, and shopping tour hostess, loves reading.

She writes both historical and contemporary western romance, as well as romantic suspense.

She lives in Melbourne, Australia, and is married with two adult children and has six grandchildren. When she's not writing, she can be found in her craft room making greeting cards.

Website: *http://www.cheryl-wright.com/*

Facebook Reader Group:
https://www.facebook.com/groups/cherylwrightauthor/

Join My Newsletter:

https://cheryl-wright.com/newsletter/
(and receive a free book)